# The Statue in Gage Park

NICOLE PATON SCHOFIELD

# DEDICATION

Dedicated to every Bramptonian who has ever skated on
the trail through beautiful Gage Park.

# CONTENTS

# ACKNOWLEDGMENTS

I would like to thank the people that spent endless time editing, proofreading, designing and publishing this book for me. As well as my family for their patience when I was absent in pursuit of my dream and I hope this encourages them to follow theirs.

# 1 BLACKOUT

The news was on in the living room but Regan and Mark Davis were too busy with their evening routines to hear it. Regan was in the kitchen cleaning up the dinner dishes while Mark was rounding up the kids for bed. It was eight o'clock and the clouds had already started to clump together blocking out the night sky as it always did just before a heavy snowfall.

Regan was tired and looking forward to getting into bed but she was suffering from the usual "night before" blues, not wanting to go to work in the morning, her stomach would twist in uncertainty and she would start questioning her life decisions.

Once the kids were clean and she had read them a story, Regan went down to the basement to retrieve the laundry and then headed to her room to fold the towels. Mark was in the kitchen packing lunches when she poked her head in, "coming to bed?" she asked. "Uh-huh," he responded licking the jam from his fingers.

He caught up with her and put the towels in the linen closet so that Regan could slip between the covers, where he then joined her. Kissing her forehead, he whispered, "good night." Regan didn't even open her tired eyes, just smiled and was asleep in no time despite her worries.

Regan lay awake in bed in the early morning hours. The rain had woken her with its incessant tapping on the bedroom window. Through the closed blinds it created an eerie feeling as if someone were trying to get in. She pulled the blankets up to her chin to block the feelings out. It didn't work.

The alarm clock on her side table was flashing which, could only mean the power had gone out at some point through the night. Regan lay on her back, staring at the white stucco ceiling feeling wide awake. Try as she might, she could not get back to sleep and if she kept moving around the disturbance was bound to wake her sleeping husband who was snoring softly next to her. As it was, Scamp, her little Jack Russell was making huffing noises every time he sensed movement. "Well maybe you should sleep on the floor like Caesar," she thought to herself. Caesar was their Great Dane who took up most of the floor space in their master bedroom.

"What if the power didn't come back on? I could end up being late for work," she worried, which just lead to more restlessness. It was no use; after about fifteen minutes of trying, she finally gave in and climbed out of the warm bed, heading for the living room, stopping only to grab the flannel throw that had been lying over her feet to keep them nice and toasty while she slept. Her feet were constantly cold so she would put the throw blanket underneath her comforter to keep them at a comfortable temperature, but she also liked that it restricted her

2

movements. Since seeing a movie about arachnophobia when she was younger, the thought of her feet being outside of any kind of cover freaked her out. Even on the hottest day in the summer she had to be covered. Especially her feet so that nothing could climb in beside her. Funnily enough, she hated to wear socks, go figure.

Caesar looked up from his expanse of floor space as she walked by. Deciding it wasn't worth the trouble of getting up, he laid his head back on the floor with a humph sound.

The house felt cold and the sound of the rain made it feel gloomy. She wrapped the flannel throw around her shoulders, shivering slightly as she made her way to the hallway, her bare feet moving silently over the plush carpet.

The first stop she made along the way was her daughter Ainslie's room. Her door was almost directly across from Regan and Mark's and stood wide open, revealing the bright pink interior contrasting with the neutral brown walls of the hallway. The little girl was huddled under her covers with her face barely showing, fast asleep and obviously toasty warm under the fluffy blankets. The pink duvet had a faux fur feel and look to it, making the girl appear as though she were a sleeping creature from a psychedelic fairy tale. Regan closed the door softly so as not to disturb the sleeping six year old.

Further down the bungalow's hall was her son Josh's room. His was on the same side of the hall as Regan and Mark's, and across from the main bathroom. The door gave a long squeak as she eased it open. The ten year old clad in pale blue flannel pajamas lay sprawled across the single bed, his blanket in a heap on the floor. She tiptoed in, and picking up the striped blue and green duvet, tucked him in making sure her son would not get cold in the night. Well, morning now. Josh turned towards his mom and smiled but his eyes were closed. She smiled to herself, "either he is having a good dream or he is too tired to open his eyes and that is his way of thanking me." She left the room trying desperately not to squeak the door with no luck. "I'll have to get Mark to oil that or something," she thought to herself, her husband was great at fixing things.

Continuing down the hall she passed the five stairs on her right that led down to the front door. The wind was howling like an animal stuck in a hunter's trap, on her other side was the door to the kitchen. She thought of putting on the kettle and having a nice warm cup of tea. The shrieking sound of the wind sent another shiver down her spine and she pulled her blanket tighter around her shoulders as if to protect her from it.

Once in the living room, she could see the whole street and through the adjoining dining room there was a wall of windows and the slider leading out to the backyard. The blinds were closed on the back wall otherwise she would see the raised deck and the stairs leading down to the main deck then beyond that the snowy covered yard with a view of the field and the hydro poles on the next street over.

The large bay window in the front gave a view almost to the bottom of the cul de sac they lived on. The rain was lashing the window and the large birch tree in the front yard was leaning precariously toward the house. That gave Regan a very uneasy feeling.

The birch had been there when they moved in; during the summer the kids would peel off the thin papery bark no matter how many times she yelled at them to stop, what they did with the bark she had no idea. The tree had grown with their family and now it towered above the roof leaving them in its shadow.

She sat on the couch and covered herself with the flannel throw. Her legs had to be curled up so that she was almost in the fetal position to ensure complete coverage; the blanket was not designed for a thirty year old, five foot five, hundred and twenty pound woman. More like a six year old child. She put her head back against the couch and watched the rain. There was something hypnotic about it hitting the glass and streaming down. The water was freezing as it slid down the window, creating a spider web effect of ice.

When she was young, her mother would sit in the dark watching the street just like this. They had a large picture window and she could watch Regan and her sister playing outside. Sometimes Regan would sit with her, just enjoying the silence. Not really sure what they were supposed to be doing, only when she was older did she realize that this was her mother's time to herself, to relax and decompress at the end of a busy day. Maybe it was a tradition and her mother had sat in the dark with her grandmother too, she had never said. And Regan had never asked. As she matured, Regan had drifted from her mother. She loved and missed her when too much time had passed, but there seemed to be an unspoken understanding that they didn't have to see each other all the time to prove the love existed. On the other hand, Regan's sister Samantha was very close with their mother; Sam spent a lot of weekends at the small house their parents both occupied now. Sam's boys had been babysat by their grandma and grandpa when they were toddlers. Regan had stayed home with her kids until they were in kindergarten.

Regan closed her eyes and drifted off to the sound of the rain, falling into a strange comatose state where she was not awake, but not quite asleep either, just somewhere in between. The rain continued to fall, the tree swayed, and the wind howled relentlessly, not allowing the trapped animal to escape.

BOOM, she woke with a start. She was awake instantly and disoriented. It sounded like a bomb went off, but she wasn't sure if she had dreamt it. Her gaze turned toward the sound. It took her a minute for her eyes to adjust and to recall why she was on the couch in the living room. The noise had come from the back window she got up in time to separate the blinds and see an electrical pole crashing to the ground in the field a couple of streets over, its metallic cables flailing wildly as if they were tentacles that had just come to life. The force of the pole collapsing pulled down another pole and another until they were all falling like dominoes. BOOM, BOOM,BOOM, she was shaking from the shock, adrenaline spiking through her body. The noise was so loud that there was no hope of anyone sleeping through it.

Scamp appeared at her side, barking. "Shhh, you stupid dog," she said picking up the little canine and putting her hand around his snout trying to shut his mouth for him. Behind her came a very deep "WOOF!" She turned in time to see Caesar trot up to the back window. "Oh, Jesus," she muttered followed by a stern "quiet Caesar." He sat looking at her with those big sad eyes. He always looked so sad and the guilt from disciplining him was almost too much for Regan. Sometimes she thought he was slow while others he surprised her with his intelligence. He stayed quiet.

What time was it? She put Scamp down on the floor and instinctively went to the kitchen to see. The stove clock was dark. "Of course, you idiot," she scolded herself, "you just saw our electricity supply come down as if Paul Bunyan were out there cutting down hydro poles like trees."

Her legs were sore and cramped from how she had been sitting on the couch. She was rubbing them when Mark came into the kitchen. "What the hell was that?" He asked his hair as it always was in the morning, perfect in the front but standing straight up in the back. She couldn't understand it as he never slept on his back but this was how he woke every morning. Ainslie called it his fast hair as it looked like he was zooming along, the wind blowing his hair back.

"The electrical poles fell down." It sounded so absurd when she said it out loud, but that was what happened. Well, they more collapsed than fell. He gave her the face he made when she said something that he did not believe. That pursed lips, cocked eyebrow; head tilted to one side tell me more bullshit face. She hated that look and wanted to smack him whenever he made it. "Go look!" she said sternly pointing to the back window still bent over trying to ease the pain in her legs.

He padded through the dining room in his bare feet to the back slider as if it was a chore. Separating the blinds, he stood there in wonder.

"What the hell?" he asked softly this time to no one, not expecting an answer. Regan stood there smug for a minute while her husband of twelve years stared in silent awe at the scene outside the window. He reached for the cord and pulled the vertical blinds open revealing the chaos outside. The rain had turned to snow now and everywhere you looked, the busy street behind their house was covered in a thick sheet of ice, dotted here and there with what looked like abandoned cars that had slid off the road. There was a total of nine poles down from what they could see, overlapping each other in a haphazard heap along the field beyond the street. When his faculties returned to him, Mark went to the front window not really expecting to see anything but snow. Across the street they could see their neighbor Mr. Fulton's house, who had a giant old maple tree that had fallen onto a transformer, cracking it open like a walnut. The transformer was spewing out some black looking smoke and the tree was splintered and uprooted at its base. It was probably a good thing that it had been raining otherwise that might have been a fire.

Mark pushed gently passed Regan heading down the hallway. Initially she thought he was going to check on the kids but he turned into the bathroom. The sound that followed was the bathtub tap. "Was he running a bath right now?" she wondered to herself in disbelief. It seemed like a weird response to what he had just seen but Regan learned a long time ago that there is method to her husband's madness and not to question him.

Remembering the children, she went to Josh's room. He was still asleep! "Wow," she thought, "he can really sleep through anything!" She left him alone, but when she got to Ainslie, the little girl was crying in her bed.

The dogs went mental. They were very in tune with the emotional state of the children. Scamp jumped on her bed and was trying to lick her face while Caesar knocked over her little drawing table in an effort to reach her, sending the little crayon caddy flying. Regan went and collected her daughter lifting her into an embrace. "Baby, what's wrong?" She asked gently, moving her daughter's shoulder length dark hair out of her face. "I heard a loud noise and thought King Kong had come to get me." Regan laughed to herself and in a soft voice she said, "Remember, we talked about that? He isn't real honey." For weeks Ainslie had been petrified that King Kong would come for her after watching an old movie one Sunday afternoon. The girl that King Kong had carried away had a similar hairstyle, even though the colour was all wrong, Ainslie had still somehow identified with the woman and convinced herself she would be the next one carried off by the big ape.

Mark appeared in the doorway looking more awake. "What's going on?" he asked looking at his distraught daughter. "The noise woke her; she thought it was King Kong." Mark gave a smirk as Regan rolled her eyes, keeping Ainslie's back to them both so that she couldn't see her parents making light of her deepest, darkest fear. Many sleepless nights had been a result of the giant ape.

"Are you having a bath?" Regan asked looking at her husband questioningly. "No….," he responded looking confused. Then it dawned on him, "the power is out, not sure for how long so I thought we should fill the bathtub as a water source. The pipes might freeze and we won't be able to get it then." In recent years he had taken a real interest in survival. He had even written a little handbook that Regan dubbed Survival Tips for the Urban Idiot. As much as she wanted to laugh at him, there was a small part of her that was a little relieved that he had picked up this particular hobby. She would never let him know that though.

The first part of the handbook was entitled "Be Prepared":

The Boy Scouts were right on the money with this motto. If you have everything you need then there is nothing to worry about. Keep your car gassed up, propane in the BBQ, some candles and a lighter easily accessible; (for example the top drawer in your kitchen) 5-10 canned items in the cupboards at all times, and always have a case of water on hand. These few things should get you through a week without power and you can avoid the weird looks from your neighbors, they will never suspect you of any extreme behavior unless you want them to.

She believed the intention was to distribute the book or create a blog or something. That being said she had hoped that they would never need it but followed it loosely all the same.

She thought guiltily of the minivan sitting idle in the garage, pretty sure that it only had a quarter tank left in it, knowing that one of his rules was to make sure that the cars never fell below a quarter tank. "Oh well," she thought to herself. "I'm sure that Mark has a full tank in his car." After all, they were his rules that they lived by.

Making her way to the kitchen, she opened the cupboard doors where the canned goods were kept. Skimming the inventory she felt secure in the fact that they were well stocked with beans, ravioli, corned beef and other assorted lunch time favourites. She felt a little better knowing that the food was there, not that they were going to need it. They lived in the suburbs and the longest the power was ever out here was a few hours.

Regan heard the long creak of Josh's door followed by footsteps and the bathroom door closing. They all stood where they were listening to the boy's movements. A few minutes later the bathroom door opened and the squeak from his door could be heard again as the door closed this time.

Ainslie had stopped crying at the sound of her brother and then yelled, "Josh! Mom says King Kong isn't real!"

There was no reply from down the hall. The little girl wriggled herself down to the ground and free of her mother's grip, running down the hall to see her brother. She trusted him more than anyone in her life, and knew he would never lie to her. Unlike her parents who might say things that were untrue to put her mind at ease. She knew that they had lied to her about the Easter bunny. Josh had confirmed that there was no such thing and she had started to question everything they said as a result.

The little girl flung her brother's bedroom door open with such force that it bounced off the stopper at the baseboard before it could slam into the wall. "Hey," she said to her brother. When he tried to ignore her she climbed onto his bed and putting her arms around his neck positioned her mouth next to his ear, "Josh," she hissed in a loud whisper. "What?" came his annoyed response. "Something's going on outside," she said. "There was a loud noise like King Kong and it scared me and the snow is really deep and I don't know what the noise was and…" "Stop," he yelled at her. "Did you say snow?" Josh had only experienced one snow day in his short life but it had instilled a magical feeling in him. An impromptu day off filled with playing in the snow, hot chocolate and watching T.V. What more could any kid ask for? He climbed out of his bed and opened the plaid drapes that matched his duvet. He couldn't see outside the window since it was covered in a sheet of rippled ice obscuring the outside world. All he could see was white.

Josh ran out of his room and headed to the living room while Ainslie trailed behind him. He stopped in front of the window, surveying the scene out front of the house and then the back. His mouth hung open, he had never seen so much of the white stuff before. "White gold!" He whopped turning to Ainslie. "Do you know what this means Ains?"

His little sister looked bewildered at him, "no, what?" "Snow day!" He shouted.

"Hold on a minute," his dad was saying. "Let's check the radio before we declare today a snow day."

# 2 DAY ONE - MORNING

*A radio is imperative. You will need to know what's going on and this will give you access to the news. A hand crank radio would be best, but if it's not available, try to keep extra batteries on hand in case of emergencies The car radio would work, but let's leave the car gas and the battery on reserve in case they're needed later on. – Survival Tips for the Urban Idiot*

"Okay Bob. I guess I will see you tomorrow then." Regan hung up her cell phone while doing a little dance, excited at the prospect of having a day off. Her boss had told her to stay home because there was no power in the office, so why risk the trek? He had driven for an hour, what would usually have been a ten minute commute, and told of cars in ditches and treacherous road conditions with no sign of snow removal yet. Regan knew the city wouldn't plow until the snow stopped. No municipality wanted to blow their budget on the first snow storm of the season.

Today would not be filled with unhappy customers calling in to complain to her about their package not being received yet. She had worked as a customer service agent for a local courier company for the past five years. She knew it was time to move on to bigger and better things but it was so hard to get motivated. The kids demanded more of her time at night with homework and projects, and then there was hockey and swimming lessons to contend with. Who has the time?

The kids were both wide awake by now and running around the house chanting "snow day!" in their PJ's. Mark had dug out his solar/battery powered radio, chapter 1 in the Survival Tips for the Urban Idiot Handbook "Be Prepared" find out how bad the storm was. It turned out to be pretty bad. Schools were closed, government agencies were shut and they were asking people to stay off the roads so that emergency vehicles, snowplows and salt trucks can get through easily. There was something ominous about the radio report and when Regan looked to Mark for reassurance she could see the same uneasiness on his face that she was feeling. She thought of her parents huddled in their little farm house trapped by the snow and worry ran through her. They did have a wood stove so she knew they would be able to keep warm and even warm up food should the power not come on soon. The power would probably take longer to come back on in their neck of the woods as the focus was usually on the areas with more people, or so Regan assumed.

"OKAY!" Regan yelled to get Josh and Ainslie's attention. "No school today but also no TV." Ainslie pouted and asked "why not? I haven't been bad." Her little cherub face made it almost impossible to deny her anything. Josh piped up, "The power's out stupid! We can't do anything that uses 'lectricity." "Hey! Don't say stupid. That's not nice." Regan snapped, then turning to Ainslie she said, "Your brother is right, we can't do anything today that plugs into the wall. So let's sit in the living room and you guys give me some ideas of what to do then. We will write them down and see how much stuff we can get done today." She herded the kids into the living room and went into the kitchen to get some paper and a pen.

"Tea party!" Ainslie yelled. Josh responded with a, "lame." "How about board games?" he asked. Regan nodded returning with the pen and paper, sitting down in the same spot where she had been dosing not long before.

"A story," Ainslie added. Regan smiled at her children. This was going to be a fun day. What an adventure this was for them. When she was young the power seemed to go out a lot more. Just one thunderstorm and they would be in the dark for a couple of hours, but these days that wasn't the case. Lights would flicker occasionally, but the children had never experienced a full-fledged black out.

The next few minutes were consumed with random suggestions of Lego, mini hockey in the basement, Barbie's, baking cookies, which required a reminder that they could not use electricity for these activities. The list went on and on. When they were finished, Regan was sure they could stay busy all day.

"Mommy, I'm hungry," Ainslie said. "Okay, let's see what we can eat." And with that they were off to the kitchen.

Opening the cupboards, there was bread and peanut butter so that was their breakfast followed by chopped up bananas. "I want toast," Ainslie whined. "Remember sweetie, we can't use anything that plugs into the wall. And the toaster plugs into the wall." Another reminder needed, this might end up being a longer day then Regan thought. The little girl became sullen every time she was told they couldn't do something because it would need to be plugged in. "She might still be tired," Regan thought to herself. "That was a hell of a way to wake up."

Ainslie pouted until her mother had an idea. "Eat up your breakfast and then we'll do something really fun." She eyed her mother suspiciously and asked, "what?" "You guys go and get as many blankets and pillows as you can find and we'll make a fort in the living room." The exercise would keep them warm and building a fort would be fun for them.

Once breakfast was finished they both ran off and returned with arms full of bedding. It took them a few trips running back and forth down the hallway to get everything they needed. At one point Caesar, maybe feeling a little left, out stepped on the blanket Josh was dragging down the hall, hauling the boy down under the pile that he had been carrying. Josh didn't mind. He yelled, "Hey!" and then lovingly patted the dog on the head. Caesar just panted, happy at the attention.

They needed their dad who was the best fort builder in the land to help them. Regan cringed at the thought of the last fort he had constructed. Her living and dining room had been dismantled for a week. He had used every chair and couch, and then moved the tables out of the way too. This would mean a big clean up when the power came back on. As long as everyone was warm and occupied, it was a good thing, she told herself.

It turned out great! The couches and two of the four dining room chairs held up their king size duvet like a canopy and in the middle stood Ainslie's mini plastic basketball net to support the centre. Inside were a multitude of blankets and pillows to lie on.

Once the fort was built the kids were tired so Regan

decided it would be a good time for a story. Josh ran down the hall and reappeared with a Harry Potter book. Ainslie was too worn out to care that she didn't get to choose the book.

They all got cozy in the fort, Scamp included. Regan lay with her head at the opening so that she could have the light from the window to see the words in the book while the kids lay on either side of her in a sea of blankets and pillows. It was surprisingly comfortable.

Once they got through the first chapter Caesar appeared and lay at Regan's head. She could smell the dampness from him and he was soaked from head to toe. "Good boy," she said to the giant canine.

He had used his doggie door that Mark installed just two weeks earlier. They were convinced that Caesar was claustrophobic. He hated the little door, he never liked to be hugged, and he would panic if you tried to put any kind of doggie clothing on him much to Ainslie's dismay. Regan's suspicion seemed to be confirmed right now as he was making no attempt to enter the fort.

It was actually a good thing that Mark had installed the door. It wouldn't be pleasant to have to open any regular sized doors right now letting in the wind and the moisture. Regan wondered if they would even be able to get a door connected to the outside open at this point. After all of the wind and freezing rain they had endured last night and into this morning, she doubted it.

After another chapter Ainslie had fallen asleep and Josh was dosing so Regan whispered to her son, "I'll be right back," and slipped out of the fort, leaving them to rest. Truth be told she probably could have had a little nap too, but she wanted to see what Mark was up to. He had been absent most of the morning.

She heard some noise coming from downstairs and carefully made her way down there. It was not complete darkness until you were in the back basement, which is where they kept all of their storage. The basement door, which opened to the yard, had a small window that let in a little bit of light for her to see. Scamp must have followed her down, as he was exiting through the doggie door which played with the light even more as the flap flipped back and forth. Mark was in the back of the dank room where he had a flashlight, so she headed towards him into the blackness. He was going through one of the bins that had been stacked neatly against the wall. They kept their family memorabilia down there along with Christmas decorations and general junk next to Mark's tools. On his workbench Mark had collected two flashlights, a handful of batteries, the camping lantern and a box of strike anywhere matches.

"You seem almost excited," Regan teased him. He jumped sucking in his breath not having heard her come in. "Jeez, you scared the shit out of me." He said putting his hand against his chest and the beam directly in her face. She held up her hand to block the harsh light. "I am," he smiled down at her, repositioning the light back to the bench, "I know it will probably only be for one night, but knowing that we are prepared and will be comfortable is nice, isn't it?" She nodded and hugged him. They collected his treasure and headed back upstairs, Mark leading the way picking his steps carefully using the flashlight and Regan holding onto the back of his sweater for guidance.

In the kitchen, Mark laid everything down on the table and Regan got some tea light candles out of the bottom drawer to do her part. They wanted to make sure that the kids would not be scared. With no house or street lights and an overcast night it was bound to be dark. Although, what little light they had from outside would reflect off of the snow, so they may just luck out.

Regan then went and got some clothes for the kids and changed into a t-shirt, hoodie, track pants and Mark's thick hunting socks, finishing off her ensemble with a digital sports watch. Something she hadn't worn since being attached to a cell phone for the past few years, but thought it would come in handy today. Her cell phone should be preserved for more important things. Meanwhile, Mark collected the last of the blankets from the linen closet. They would definitely be cozy that afternoon. It was just too bad they couldn't make hot chocolate and the weather was too extreme to play in the snow.

It was a little exciting. Regan was looking forward to all of them being together. Too often they got caught up in their lives. Hockey practices, swim meets, work, school. There just wasn't enough time for them to spend much of it together as a family.

They had tried to implement a family fun night a few times, where they played a board game or told stories. But it never seemed to last, always getting bumped for something more important. Well, not really more important because what's more important than family? Just a scheduling conflict that ended up dictating their plans, changing family fun night for that week and then not going back to it. Regan knew that they should spend more time together, but it was so difficult.

Josh plodded into the kitchen. "I'm bored," he announced to his parents. Regan turned to her son, ruffled his dirty blond hair and said, "okay kiddo, how about a game of UNO?" He took off without saying a word presumably to get the deck of cards from his room while Regan wandered back to the fort. She knew how much Josh loved UNO and that would change his impending mood.

Ainslie was lying on her back playing with her stuffed bunny rabbit and talking to Caesar who answered every once in a while outside the fort with either a humph or some sort of groan. She had him wrapped around her little finger.

"What's going on in here?" her mother asked, petting Caesar as she entered the fort on all fours again. "Noothin'," was Ainslie's reply. "Josh went to get some UNO cards," her mom reported. Ainslie smiled at her mom and sitting up she said, "I love today mommy." Regan smiled as well and said, "I do too because I get to spend some time with you guys!" The little girl hugged her bunny close to her and squeezed it as hard as she could.

Josh returned with the cards and they got down to business. He shuffled and dealt, trying to do some fancy moves to show off his skills. Five games later Josh had won three, Ainslie won one and the last one ended in some silliness where Scamp ran into the fort scattering the cards everywhere and Josh declared Caesar the winner for being a good boy. That was the end of that.

The morning had flown by when Regan looked at her watch, it was already 11:55 "Okay, who's hungry?" She asked the kids before they got out of hand. "I am!" Announced Ainslie, followed by Josh's, "me too!"

"Well alright let's go see what we can find," and with that the three of them headed for the kitchen where Mark was still hunkered down.

"Hi daddy," Ainslie said beaming at her father. "Hey there princess," Mark replied lifting his daughter up onto the table beside all of his collectibles. "Whatcha doin'," the little girl asked. "Well, I am going to make sure that we have enough light tonight and that we are nice and warm. "When will the lights come back on?" she inquired. It caught Mark off guard, but he was used to Ainslie's directness. "I really don't know honey, but I am pretty sure it will be sometime today."

With that Mark turned the little hand crank radio on. "Let's see what they are saying on the news." he suggested. "ugh, I hate the news," Josh declared rolling his big blue eyes.

"You know Joshy, at a time like this it is important to listen to the news so that you know what is happening. Like this morning, they were telling people that it's too dangerous to drive." "What if mom hadn't heard that? She could have still tried to go to work and gotten hurt or stuck."

Josh didn't answer. He knew that it wasn't really a question. The radio buzzed to life. "Possibly ten inches of snow overnight. For those of you without power, the utility companies are working to restore it as soon as possible. Quite a few hydro poles have collapsed under the weight of the ice and snow, making restoration a bit tricky."

"Who wants corned beef…" "SHHHH," Mark shushed his wife. He was listening intently to the radio. Regan recoiled at the noise coming from her husband. "sorry," she muttered under her breath at him turning back to the counter to make sandwiches. "So just try and keep warm and dry folks, because it looks like this storm is going to be hanging around for a little while."

Mark snapped the power button to off on the radio. He knew that they needed to use it as little as possible. Even though it was a hand crank he didn't know how good it was. The kids had bought it for him for Christmas one year so it was a cheaper version of what he would have liked. But it was serving the purpose right now.

Regan opened and shut the fridge as quickly as possible, snatching the loaf of bread from the top shelf. The house was still relatively warm and she didn't want the fridge to heat up as a result.

They feasted on corned beef sandwiches with cucumber slices on the side. The bread only had a few more slices left in the bag. Regan knew there was another loaf in the freezer that they could take out, but a nice hot meal would do them all good for supper. How were they going to do that she wondered. With no electricity, their stove would not work and the barbecue might as well have been a hundred miles away! You couldn't even see it out the back door anymore, pushed all the way up against the far side of the deck, being covered in layer after layer of falling and blowing snow.

"Plates in the sink," Regan called as the kids tried to walk out of the kitchen, leaving behind their lunch mess. They both groaned but came back to the table scraping the food remnants into the garbage and noisily putting the dishes in the sink.

Regan peered out the kitchen window. The sky was grey with complete cloud coverage. You could only see about a foot from the window now. The backyard was completely blanketed in snow, the deck just a random mound. It did look pretty though. Regan always loved the renewed look that snow provided. It was like a reset for nature.

Gone was the icy glaze that she had seen that morning but it lurked beneath the surface almost menacingly. A path would need to be shoveled for Caesar and Scamp outside the basement door. That could be done in a little while once it lightened up, that way the dogs wouldn't get cut from the sharp edges when their paws punched through the snowy crust.

Just last year the larger dog had been loping around in similar conditions, although not as extreme,  only to slice the back of his left leg open. He ended up needing five stitches to close the wound. Winter can be a dangerous time of year for everybody. After getting hurt Regan had bought Caesar some booties that he promptly ate, pooping vinyl for days afterwards. She never did find the matching hat….

# 3 DAY ONE - AFTERNOON

*In the event of a power outage, no matter what the season, the most important thing is to remain calm. Keep your loved ones close and encourage them to keep calm as well. In our modern age I think we tend to panic a little prematurely. —Survival Tips for the Urban Idiot*

Ainslie and Josh were sprawled out on the floor of the fort playing Candy Land nicely while Regan was curled up in the only recliner that hadn't been claimed for the little tent, reading a book that she had meant to start ages ago. Mark had given it to her two Christmases past. The house was so peaceful, with the exception of Mark was obsessively trying to find items in the house that they might need, he wanted to be ready for anything, ignoring the possibility that there were circumstances that he couldn't be accounting for in his what if scenarios.

His thoughts turned to the garage and the two vehicles parked in there. His car was on empty and he was wondering how much gas Regan had in the minivan. She was not always as diligent as she claimed to be. He had meant to stop on the way home last night, but he just wanted to get home, breaking his own rule of never leaving the cars low on gas, especially in the winter. He was pretty sure that the little red canister he kept on the shelf in the garage that he used for the lawn mower had some fuel in it. How much, he could not say. The thought of digging out the driveway as a means of escape seemed pointless when the streets beyond hadn't been plowed. He might get out of the driveway only to be stuck in the street. If the roads stayed that way it wouldn't matter how much gas was in either car, they weren't going anywhere.

Mark kept looking out the kitchen window expecting to see the snow stop, but it didn't seem to be letting up out there at all. Large fluffy clumps of snow were constantly falling. And now they were calling for another ten inches overnight. "What would that look like?" He wondered. Outside, there was no sign of anything man made. The snow had blanketed everything, turning the world into white bumps and hills as far as the eye could see, with only the spots of brown from the trees poking through and interrupting the effect. On some of them you could still see green, but very little. For the most part, they were jagged sticks encased in ice being pulled down by the weight of the frozen water entrapping each limb, the falling snow settling on top of the ice adding more weight for the poor trees to bear. They looked grotesquely disfigured pointing at unnatural angles. And the ice gave them an impression of being skinny, malnourished beings as opposed to the full proud pines that they usually resembled.

At first, this had been an exciting adventure and Mark had felt ready, but after hearing the weather report he was starting to feel a little anxious. The family needed to be looked after and it was his job to make sure they were okay, but he wasn't sure what that would mean. The unknown was always the worst for him. He liked to be in control and work out every possible outcome but he wasn't able to do that this time.

"Calm down Mark," he said to himself, "the first rule of survival is to not panic." Now he knew why it was the first rule. He felt he was ready for anything, yet the feeling of uncertainty still managed to creep in. "That's right," he said to himself, and taking a deep breath, he gave his head a little shake. "I've got everything we could possibly need." He surveyed the items on the table one more time, taking a mental inventory. Then, he headed out of the kitchen and into the living room, attempting to leave the burden that had been plaguing him all morning behind.

He needed a distraction. "Who wants to play crazy 8's?" he asked the room. Regan looked up and smiled. Ainslie squealed, "I'm winning! Can we finish this game daddy?" It was more of a demand than a question. And Mark knew better than to get in the way of his daughter's victory. She was a poor winner. He knew that, and was reminded of that fact right now. He made a mental note that he and Regan should help Ainslie with that. The little girl knew how to accept a loss though, she was gracious in defeat. That must have come from having an older brother that seemed to beat her at everything.

Once Ainslie was crowned the queen of Candy Land-Regan had her suspicions that Josh had thrown it in order to speed up the process-they all huddled into the fort for a game of Crazy 8's Countdown.

Outside, the wind howled and the snow continued to fall. Up and down Sunset Place, not a soul could be seen. Most of the houses looked abandoned due to the frosted windows and un-shoveled driveways. The radio had warned people with heart conditions of the heavy snow accumulating and the risks of shoveling. No sound of snowplows or sirens reached the quiet street. It was as if they were in a bubble, the snow acting as an insulator.

Trees continued to be padded with layer after layer of ice and snow. The branches inched closer to the ground with every snowflake that fell. The maple that had fallen in Mr. Fulton's yard was now just a large bump in the snow, indistinguishable from the cars that had been left out on their neighbors' driveways. At least the snow had doused the smoldering wood, eliminating any chance of a fire from the transformer it had fallen across.

The birch in the front yard of Mark and Regan's house was no longer a risk having succumbed to the heavy ice that had formed down its trunk. The soft tree was almost folded in half to Regan and Mark's relief. If it had landed on the roof it may have caused some damage and exposed them to the raging storm outside. There would have been no way to patch the roof. Mark didn't have the material, and to climb a ladder in the wind and cold would have been treacherous. Even just leaving the house right now would be risky because of the likelihood of being frostbitten.

After a few card games, the kids spent the rest of the afternoon playing mini hockey and fetch in the basement with the dogs. The front windows in the basement gave enough light for the kids to feel comfortable going down there. And the temperature wasn't much different than the living room. Still, Regan had told them to put on gloves and toques to be sure.

Scamp kept on going out through the doggie door in the back basement, and bringing in chunks of snow that he would lie on the floor and lick for his enjoyment. Every time the little dog went outside a gust of frigid air would invade the house. They couldn't lock it though, or else the dogs might get hurt running into the door thinking it was open.

Caesar seemed quite happy just to lie around with his family when he wasn't stealing the little ball the kids were using to play mini hockey with. The house seemed smaller with all of them trapped in it. They were not the type of family to stay indoors. In the winter they would play in the snow, go tobogganing, ski, or even just go for walks around the neighborhood to see the beauty of the season. While in the summer, the kids would play in the sandbox, run through the sprinkler or kick the soccer ball around the backyard.

Regan and Mark started talking about dinner plans. "It would be really nice if we could have something warm." Regan was saying. "I know," was Mark's reply, "but how are we supposed to do that?" asked Mark. "Going out in that storm is too dangerous. Do you want to go out there and barbecue? Because I sure don't," he wrapped his arm around her waist. "There's even a chance that the barbecue might not work." He said pressing his forehead to hers, "The lines could be frozen. We have plenty to eat without having to do something like that," That was the end of it. Regan supposed he was right. She didn't want to go out and cook in this either, risking frostbite or wind burn, but she couldn't shake the chill she seemed to have. He drew her to him and kissed her lightly on the lips. She shivered and releasing her he reached for her hands. "You're cold," he said. Pulling her gently to the front door, he went into the little wooden box her mom had given them as a gift from one of the many craft shows that she had attended. They kept all of the winter hats and gloves in there and he found some fuzzy pink mittens that Regan had received from his mother the year before for Christmas. "Come on put these on, you know you want to," he taunted her dangling them a foot in front of her face. She snatched the ugly mitts from his hands while glaring at him. Having vowed to never wear the gloves as they were tacky, she reluctantly slipped them onto her slightly numb hands. They were ugly, but they were also fur-lined and warm Now she was being forced to eat her words. They didn't taste good! "There are other ways to stay warm," he whispered into her ear. She shoved him playfully out of her way and went into the living room to warm up with a blanket. He just stood there grinning at her watching as she walked away.

Their dinner was a round of peanut butter and jelly sandwiches to the kid's disappointment, followed by a can of peaches that Regan found in the cupboard and topped with some whip cream. That brought the kids around. They ate in the fort on paper plates that had been left over from somebody's birthday party. Some colorful character was giving a thumbs-up from a neon "Happy Birthday" script. Regan didn't feel like messing around washing dishes by hand. The breakfast and lunch dishes were still sitting in the sink. "They can go in the dishwasher and I will put it on tomorrow when the power comes back on," she thought to herself. Her days of hand washing were far behind her. She could remember when her and Mark had just gotten married and their first apartment didn't have a dishwasher. It was fine, but after a couple of weeks she couldn't take it anymore. Not only does a dishwasher wash your dishes it also hides them. Nobody ever mentions that as part of their functionality. She would get so annoyed by the constant pile of dishes that would accumulate in the sink. They saved up and bought a countertop dishwasher and never looked back!

It was five o'clock when it started to get dark and Regan and Mark lit about twenty of the tea light candles. They gave off a surprising amount of light and they had a bag of a hundred so they could afford to be generous with them. The house beyond their little fort was pitch-black just an hour afterward, making Regan a little uneasy. Scamp would occasionally lift his head and stare off, hearing something that was far beyond their abilities. Whenever he did this, Regan would try desperately to hear what had disturbed the canine, but was never able. Peering into the dark each time didn't help either. It only made her see things that weren't really there.

The wind seemed to get louder in the dark and for some reason Caesar thought it was a good idea to howl along with it. "HOOOWWWWLL," he cried into the night. Everyone jumped at the sound of his call, then laughed at the dog uncomfortably. "Be quiet," Regan told him. He obliged sheepishly, giving her the saddest face she could have imagined. He then laid his big head back down on the floor, making her feel as though his fun had been spoiled. She ran her hand over the short fur on his back to make herself feel better.

They had decided it would be best for all of them to stay in the living room and sleep in the fort tonight. The kids thought that was a great idea and chatted excitedly about it while they organized the space, piling up pillows and laying claim to blankets, chasing Scamp out of the fort while they got it ready.

Mark played chess with Josh while Ainslie and Regan watched. Regan braided Ainslie's hair, while the little girl chattered away about ponies or school even the snow, whatever popped into her head. Josh had managed to beat his father at the game for the first time in his life. He was so excited he jumped up almost taking down the fort in his haste. Then they switched and Ainslie played her dad while Josh attempted to braid his mom's hair. It didn't quite go as smoothly as when Regan did Ainslie's but Josh was quite proud of the end result tying it with a red ribbon so that it wouldn't come undone. Ainslie patiently took defeat over and over again; it was as if it only made her more determined to win.

After chess they played eye spy and the kids asked about how Regan and Mark had met. "Well," said Mark, "I was at your Uncle Ted's wedding and your mommy was there." Ted was Mark's older brother. "Yes, I had gone with a friend from work who didn't have a date," Regan added.

"I saw your mommy in her pretty purple dress." "It was violet," Regan interrupted. "And I just knew that I wanted to meet her. So I gathered up my courage, walked up to her, and asked her if she wanted to dance. And she said…..No!" The kids gasped and Regan giggled. Then she carried on the story from that point. "I had twisted my ankle and couldn't dance. I had my big swollen foot hidden under the table and sat there all night," she explained. "I told your dad that I couldn't, I had injured my foot while walking up some complicated stairs." The kids laughed knowing how clumsy their mother was, "so he asked if he could sit with me and I said of course. He made me laugh and we chatted all night. It was as if we had known each other all along and we were never apart from then on," she beamed at her husband.

"Yup, that's how you do it Josh. Wait for them to be hurt so that they can't run away. If she was sick that would have worked too, really any weakened condition." They all laughed. "What did you talk about?" Josh asked. "Umm, I asked her what she liked to do, if she had any family. And other stuff like that." His dad responded. Josh seemed to be taking mental notes and Mark looked at his wife with a smile on his face and his eyebrows raised as if to say, "I think he has a young lady he wants in his life." She smiled back. Time had gone by so fast. It seemed like yesterday they had brought Josh home from the hospital, his little face pink from crying. He had suffered from colic and was a very unhappy baby for the first six months of his life.

They all sat quietly listening to the wind again; it had become a high pitch scream. It was wild outside. An unsettling feeling coveted the room for a few minutes with the uncertainty of their situation. Then Josh broke it, "Mom will you read to us some more?" he asked handing her the book they had started earlier that day. "Sure," she replied, "let's all get cozy."

Regan made sure the kids put on socks and changed into the warm pajamas she had collected for them and left on the couch. They had three warm blankets to keep the heat in and mini knit gloves if they wanted them. Mark was wearing his fleece track pants, a t-shirt, sweatshirt and socks while Regan wore her fleece pajamas with the bottom of the pant legs tucked into a pair of Mark's hunting socks.

Once dressed, they climbed under the covers in the safety of the fort. This time, Mark lay on the right side of the fort closest to the make-shift blanket wall, then Ainslie, Regan, and Josh at the other side. Scamp was curled up at Ainslie's feet and Caesar was just beyond him outside of the fort. They were all cozy and warm.

"Okay, everybody ready?" Regan asked while positioning a candle on a little plastic stool they had brought in as a make-shift card table, she put the stool just behind her pillow so that the little candle gave off a soft glow; just enough to read by and it wouldn't keep anyone awake, or start a fire. "Yes," they all answered. Ainslie and Josh cuddled into her while Mark leaned on his elbow ready to hear the story.

It took five chapters before they were all asleep. Regan checked her watch and found that it was only nine o'clock. It had been an exciting day and they were all worn out. She lay on the ground listening to the sounds of her children sleeping softly; even Mark was snoring. All of a sudden, a sense of dread welled up inside her making her feel panicky. Anxiety of the situation was troubling her and she was starting to worry about the power being off for such a long time. "What is wrong with me?" she scolded herself, blowing out the little candle. "It has only been a day. I'm sure when we wake up in the morning the power will be back on and everything will go back to normal." She tried to go to sleep but sleep wouldn't come.

Through the night, she listened to the wind howl and the gritty sound of the icy snow beating against the windows. In her sleepy mind, the wind started to sound like the cries of her neighbors. All along the street she imagined them screaming for help. Anxiety was rising in her throat like bile, creating the feeling of her windpipe closing on her and restricting her air flow. She had to calm herself down, visions of her parents huddled by a small fire with blue skin and icicles hanging from their noses danced through her mind, "it's just the wind, it's just the wind.." she repeated over and over. Eventually, with a pillow held over her ears to block the eerie sounds she, was able to succumb to the exhaustion    and    fell    into    a    deep    sleep.

# 4 DAY TWO - MORNING

*More often than naught, your power will come back on within 24 hours. It will be the top priority of the municipality that you live in to get that electricity flowing down the cable highways and into your homestead. Try to remember that. Help is more than likely on its way!*
*— Survival Tips for the Urban Idiot*

The temperature had dropped through the night, but they hadn't felt it too much, staying comfortable enough in their make-shift dog pile, complete with dogs. Scamp was curled up next to Josh. Regan could feel the little dog's warmth radiating through the blankets and Caesar had worked his way into the tent just a bit. His huge head had one of Ainslie's tiny feet on top of it. It amazed Regan what the little girl could get away with when it came to Caesar. Regan noted he had made sure to leave his long legs sticking out for a quick getaway in case claustrophobia kicked in she supposed.

The morning light had started to come in through the windows, but the snow had collected on the exterior ledge blocking half of their view to the street. Regan couldn't see outside as a result and decided to get up for a closer look. She wrestled herself free from blankets and children. Somehow during the night Josh had turned horizontal and lay across her and she knew that Ainslie had punched or kicked her as her upper thigh felt bruised.

They would have to start getting up soon. The house didn't seem too cold, definitely colder than the day before, but the furnace must have kicked on during the night. There is no way the house would have stayed warm if it hadn't. Or so Regan thought.

As she crawled out of the fort, she could feel the stiffness in her legs and back. She stood up and stretched, twisting at the waist hoping to work out the kinks and tightness. She was tired and knew that it would be a long day. Sometimes at work she felt close to nodding off from boredom. If there weren't a lot of calls, there wasn't much to do. Sure you could always offer help to your Manager and then have some inane project thrust upon you. Regan would rather look busy then be bogged down with nonsense work. Today, she might actually be in danger of falling asleep at her desk. Envisioning her eyes closing and head lolling forward then smacking off the laminate desk, perhaps she could stay awake after all.

At five foot five, she was too short to see over the snow that had accumulated on the window ledge even on her tiptoes, and she couldn't bang on the window or open it to make the snow fall without waking everyone, so she left it for now. Grabbing her watch from the little stool she had used for the candle light, she saw it was almost eight in the morning. They should be up and moving as school started at eight thirty but something stopped Regan from waking her kids, sure that today of all days lateness would be forgiven.

Walking to the wall she flicked the light switch for the hallway up, nothing happened. So she did it again, down then up, still nothing. She went into the kitchen and the clock was still dark. Her stomach dropped, the power was still off. What did this mean? Would they have to face another whole day without the comfort of electricity? Did she have to go to work? Were schools open? Too many thoughts swirled around in her head and panic started to take a hold of her. She needed to sit down and get a grip. With that she scrambled to one of the kitchen chairs and plunked herself down.

"Yesterday wasn't so bad," she told herself, but the uncertainty was what bothered her. If the radio reports could give them an indication when the power would be back on…

She turned the radio on with the volume very low so as not to disturb her family who were still sleeping in the other room:

"Well, it looks like we got a little around 13 inches last night. I hope all of you are staying warm out there. I've been stuck at the station since 5 am yesterday. There's no way to get out of the parking lot, and the surrounding roads have yet to be plowed. We are being told to let everyone know that they are working on restoring the power; not sure when it will be back on, there are roughly four million homes still without power in the tristate area. If you don't need to go outside, DON'T! It is still a real mess out there and everything is still shut anyway." She turned it off.

They still weren't saying when it would be back on. Picking up her cell from the kitchen table she tried calling her boss but it went straight to voicemail so she texted him.

'News says to stay home, still no sign of a plow.' When she sent the message it grayed out and a little red exclamation point appeared next to it indicating that the message hadn't been delivered. The last thing she wanted to do was go out in this weather but she needed her job. She looked at her signal; two bars appeared in the upper right hand screen, so it wasn't her phone that was the problem, "maybe Bob had run out of juice." Calling back she left a voicemail reiterating what her text had said, she was covered for missing today. Turning off the phone she put it back where it was.

The snow was beautiful out of the back window. Even without the sun shining it glistened and sparkled. Everything was covered and the white powder hadn't been touched by any human or animal. It took her back to her childhood when she would go outside and play for hours. Her favourite part of a fresh snowfall had been to go in the backyard before anything had disturbed the new dusting and pretend that she was the only one for miles on a North Pole expedition.

She hated to leave once she was out there; only abandoning her solace when nature called or hunger took hold. She had no memory of ever being forced back inside as a result of feeling too cold. Her older sister used to hang her wet socks by the electric fire to dry them and make Regan a cup of hot chocolate after playing outside. Their parents wouldn't be home from work for about an hour after the girls got home from school. They were latch key kids, letting themselves into their home at the end of the day and starting dinner for the family when they got old enough.

The thought of her sister brought Regan out of her reverie. Samantha was a couple of years older and lived fairly close to Regan, but she had gone to Florida with her husband and Regan's nephews two days prior for a family vacation. Their timing couldn't have been better.

A sense of longing came over her at the thought of her sister and Regan picked up her phone again and tried sending her sister a text. This time the little message turned green assuring her that it had gotten through. Almost instantly Sam was replying. "Is it as bad as they are saying?" she asked. "Yes," Regan replied and told her sister of never-ending snow that was still falling and the lack of electricity. Regan knew she should keep it short but there was some comfort in knowing that she could reach someone out in the world.

"I can't reach mom and dad," Sam's words were like a punch to the gut. The twisted picture from last night resurfaced in Regan's brain. Her parents lived about an hour to the south of the city and she had hoped they were not affected by the storm having heard no mention of their county on the radio but what she heard this morning changed things. Neither parent owned a cell phone so it would be impossible to reach them right now. "Keep trying," was Regan's response. "They are working on restoring the power so they might just be out right now." Sam said she would and Regan told her she would text her later in the day. With that the phone was turned off to preserve the battery. They still had Mark's once hers was dead.

As much as she loved the snow this was not something to play around with. Only the roof of the shed could be seen peeking out a foot from the drift that covered the little building. She had never seen anything like this in her thirty five years of living in the suburbs. Who knew what hazards lay under that snow, and with no heat, the clothes worn while exploring would end up soaked and stay soaked, eventually freezing without heat to dry them.

Mark came into the kitchen yawning. "Did you check the news?" he asked. "Yes," Regan replied. "Still no power, they're not saying when it will be back and look at this. Is this not crazy? I have never seen this much snow." She blurted, throwing her hands towards the window and turning to glare at the backyard as if it would melt away from fear at her stare.

He came up behind her and wrapped his arms around her waist, then softly said into her ear, "it's beautiful isn't it?" then kissed her on the cheek releasing her from his grip.

"It's nerve-wracking is what it is," she muttered to herself but he heard what she had said. "What's wrong? You love the snow," he said turning her to face him. "I just…" she wasn't sure how to put her feelings into words. "I'm scared, I texted Sam and she hasn't heard from my parents," was all she said but it was more than that. "We'll be okay," he cut in, "we have everything that we could possibly need, and I doubt that the storm reached them. It probably blew right on past. And if it didn't they are probably better off than we are with that wood stove of theirs," he said nodding at her and looking into her eyes to show that he meant every word he was saying, even if he wasn't sure. Would her dad have been able to get to the wood pile? Mark doubted it. They kept it at the side of the carport which was about twenty yards from the house. He could only hope that before the storm had gotten too bad they had loaded up on logs for the fire and not waited until the wood was damp. If they had waited they wouldn't be able to dry it out and the wood stove would be of no use to them.

"I know," she replied, but what she wanted to say was that she had a bad feeling, that her anxiety had kept her up half the night that she thought she could hear the neighbors screaming for her help and she had been dogged by visions of her parents in peril. Instead she kept it to herself and let Mark walk out of the kitchen feeling like he had reassured her. Why should she burden him with her uncertainty? It already felt like he was putting a lot on himself.

As he left the kitchen he grabbed a bottle from the case of water by the door and felt a stab of pain knife through his forehead, "I would kill for a cup of coffee right now," he thought to himself. The dull ache of a caffeine headache had started right between his eyes and the warm liquid would have kept the chill he felt at bay. Instead, he sipped the bottle of water he had grabbed from the kitchen and rubbed at the pain. The water was room temperature, "blech." The only time he drank water was when it was at sub-zero temperatures or had ice cubes bobbing around in it. "We could put a few bottles outside," he thought to himself. "That might make us feel even colder though and the act of opening the door won't help the temperature in the house." He frowned at the bottle.

His thoughts turned to Regan's parents. Would they be okay in that little house? They lived in a small, single-bedroom house in the country. Their closest neighbor was a good half a mile down the road, impossible to get to in this snow. They may as well be on the other side of the world. Did they store food? Mark didn't know. They had struck him as minimalists; never buying any more than needed, a result of pension living, you couldn't live beyond your means. He hoped that they were okay. They were good people, always treating him like one of their own and if something were to happen to them it would deal a severe blow to his family. His own parents were in England so he didn't speak to them as much as he would have liked, but at least he knew they were out of harm's way right now.

Looking out the front window, he banged on the wooden frame, sending the snow that had been blocking the scene outside plummeting to the ground below with a soft thump, clearing the view to the street. The snow was swirling and casting shadows, creating images that were there one minute and gone the next. It was kind of freaky and sent a shiver up his spine. "You can't help but feel vulnerable when the future is uncertain," Mark thought he saw something on four legs run past but when he looked closer he knew his eyes and the snow were just playing tricks on him. He leaned his head against the frigid glass in an effort to gain relief from the pain increasing there, balancing his bottle of water on the internal ledge. He closed his eyes and lowered his shoulders trying to will the pain away.

After a few minutes, his forehead numb, Mark lifted his head and stared out into the white. The glare brought tears to his eyes as the snow reflected what little sunlight they had. The movement of the snow was almost hypnotic and Mark found it hard to look away.

Ainslie came in munching on an Ambrosia apple. Mark turned to look at his daughter. The apple looked huge in her little hand. "Is that an organic apple?" he asked her. She just shrugged and took another bite. "Did you wash it?" She stared blankly at her father as if he were speaking another language. When she pulled the apple from her mouth a little white tooth had been left behind. "AHHHHHHH!" she screamed at the site of her tooth sticking out of the apple. Mark rushed to her, "it's okay." He soothed, "you just lost your tooth." She calmed down and realized what had happened. "I thought it was a worm," she pouted, still shaken. Josh had come in to see what the commotion was about. "Hey Ainslie, put that under your pillow tonight and the tooth fairy will come." Mark could have hit him. They didn't have any cash in the house to play tooth fairy. Regan had also created a tradition of giving a new toothbrush on these special occasions and there was no chance of her doing that. Josh gave his dad a big smile. As if to say see I am old enough to play along. Mark couldn't help himself and smiled back, how was Josh to know his parents weren't equipped to play imaginary characters twenty four seven. They would just have to wing it tonight.

Ainslie pulled the little tooth from her apple and went running off to show her mother. She found Regan in the girl's bedroom going through the drawers looking for warm socks. Ainslie's feet had a tendency to be icy cold when the house was warm so she wanted to make sure her daughter wouldn't lose any toes due to frostbite. She settled on some fluffy, purple socks that had been stuffed in the back of her top drawer that had probably never even been touched.

"Look mommy!" Ainslie held up her prize so that her mother could see. Regan had to pull back and squint to see what Ainslie was jabbering on about. "Oh, is that a tooth?" Regan asked, recognition dawning on her face as she tried to figure out what she was holding. "Yes," she answered proudly. "Awesome," Regan said not sounding very thrilled at all by this latest news. "Let me see your mouth?" Regan asked, Ainslie opened her mouth and let out an "AH," opening her mouth as wide as she could and sticking out her tongue. Regan just wanted to make sure the gap where the tooth had been was not bleeding. Everything looked okay. Regan closed her daughter's mouth for her. The little girl had over done it as usual. She was such a ham.

"Josh says the tooth fairy will come tonight," Ainslie

reported. Regan stiffened and stared back at her daughter realizing that she didn't have anything to put under her daughter's pillow as proof that the tooth loving little imp had paid her a visit. Regan would have to get creative. "Can you please put these on?" Regan handed her daughter the pair of thick socks to change the subject, and left the bedroom heading back to the living room wracking her brain for an idea. "Maybe she will forget," she thought to herself and then as if on cue Ainslie ran past her with fairy wings on her back and a wand in her hand. "Hey Josh," she hollered, "Let's play tooth fairy." And with that Regan knew she had to come up with something.

Regan found Mark in the kitchen. He was chopping and peeling carrots and had the bread, peanut butter and jam on the counter. Regan made a face at him. "Don't start," he said. "If the weather breaks this afternoon maybe we can try the barbecue for something different to eat. We are all sick of sandwiches but for now we just need to eat." She made a motion in front of her lips as if she were turning a lock and then throwing away the key to indicate she wasn't saying anything. He just shook his head.

They all sat cross legged in the fort with their sandwiches. The kids had protested loudly and Ainslie sat staring at her plate with a sullen look as if it were poison. "Come on," Regan chided. "We need to eat and once the storm quiets we can have something warm." Ainslie looked at her mother in disbelief and raised the sandwich to her mouth taking a bite. Josh scarfed his down even though he complained. "Hunger will always win," Regan thought to herself.

# 5 DAY TWO - AFTERNOON

*When caught in a winter storm, water is easy to come by. Besides that case of water that I recommended earlier, you can melt the snow. Yes, snow is just frozen water and I wouldn't normally condone drinking it but in a pinch what else are you going to do. Just avoid the yellow stuff! – Survival Tips for the Urban Idiot*

Someone pounded on the front door desperately which sent Scamp into a barking frenzy, and startled the rest of the family. "Who could possibly be out in this?" Regan wondered to herself giving her husband a questioning look which he returned.

Mark headed for the door while Regan, Ainslie, Josh and Caesar left what remained of their lunches to stand at the top of the stairs. Mark braced himself and gave the door a mighty yank, expecting it to be frozen shut, which of course it was.

It gave a loud crack as he forced it open, the ice shattering under the strain. He disappeared from view for an instant and then had Mr. Fulton the neighbor from across the road by the arm, pulling him into the house through the deep snow and pushing the door closed with all of his might to shut the wind and weather out as quickly as possible.

Poor Mr. Fulton's face was as red as an apple. He pulled off his lime green gloves, exposing his wrinkled hands. Nobody on the street knew how old he was, but if Regan were to guess, she would say in his late seventies. He had a slim build, a bit of a stoop across the shoulders, and his face always seemed to be twisted into a snarl. Upon entering the house his glasses fogged up with the drastic temperature change.

He had been living here long before anyone else on the street, but Regan never saw any family coming or going. It was rumored that he had been married to a lovely woman, but she became very ill and died two years before they had moved in and as a result he had turned into a bitter old man. The little wooden sign at the foot of his driveway stated the house was "The Fulton's" but there was only one Fulton that remained.  Every street has someone that the neighborhood kids are scared of, Mr. Fulton was theirs. Regan had even heard her own kids challenging each other to run across his lawn or touch his mailbox to her chagrin.

Regan was not a fan of his, but Mark seemed to like him enough, often chatting at the foot of the driveway in summer while Mr. Fulton made his nightly rounds stalking the sidewalk at dusk each night, sending the kids scurrying home. "He's harmless," Mark would say, "Just a lonely old man."

But Regan didn't buy that. The way he walked around as if he owned Sunset Place. That's what irritated her the most, his criticizing the length of someone's grass or the fact that the Christmas lights were still up in February. Who was he to say? They had never had a neighborhood meeting or implied in any way that the street had a code of conduct that the residents had to adhere to. They weren't even a close-knit street, Regan knew the names of the neighbors on both sides of their house, but had never been in their houses and most conversations were just a quick hello. She liked it that way, nobody in her business.

"Arthur, what are you doing out there?" Mark gasped. "It isn't safe." The older man with his rosy cheeks smiled and said, "Thought I would check on the neighbors." Regan just watched from the top of the stairs looking down on both of the men while both kids hid behind her. Even Caesar seemed to shiver, but that might have been from the cold they had just let in.

Regan resented the fact that Mark had opened the door. The cold had whipped through the house and now there was a pile of snow at the front door that seemed to intensify the chill that now hung in the air. What did she expect him to do? Leave the old guy out in the snow?

Scamp took one look at the old man and ran away. "I know how you feel," Regan thought to herself. Caesar just sat beside her at the top of the stairs. She let her hand fall on top of the beasts head to reassure him that this was the proper place to be in that moment.

"Well, come in, come in," Mark welcomed him brushing the snow off of his jacket onto the gathering pile on the floor. Regan was staring at the frozen water growing by the minute on her floor that no one in her family had created.

Mr. Fulton took off his hat revealing his white wispy hair that was standing straight up. There wasn't much left up there and what remained looked baby fine. He stuffed his gloves in one of the pockets of his parka. Taking off his jacket, he hung it on the hook at the front door as if he lived there and had done it a million times before. By the time he was finished Arthur Fulton stood at the landing in a brown knit cardigan with what looked like three shirts underneath and brown cords protecting his legs. It didn't seem like that was enough to keep anyone warm in this weather. Regan could not remember the old man ever stepping foot into her home. He stomped his boots and then removed them, leaving more snowy remnants at the front door. Each snowflake that fell fueled Regan's hatred for this man.

Regan hoped her face was succeeding in masking her upset because with each move he made, the old man was making her more and more uneasy. She turned to head back into the living room where the kids were currently stationed. Caesar scrambled alongside her to keep up.

Mr. Fulton climbed the few steps to the landing and peered into the living room, having to take a moment at the top of the stairs as he was out of breath after his excursion across the street. "Well, what's all this then?" he puffed pointing to the fort and trying to sound a little too friendly in Regan's opinion. "We made it for the kids, you know, trying to have a little bit of fun so they don't get scared," Mark whispered the last part.

Mr. Fulton's eyes rested on the paper plates leavened with what was left of lunch. Regan quickly cleared up the mess and put it in the kitchen. "We don't know how long this storm is going to last," she thought to herself. "We are not giving away any of our food!" She instantly felt ashamed that she could think such a thing. He just seemed to bring out the worst in her. She tried to look at him like a feeble old man, but it didn't work. This was a basic instinctual feeling she had, too primal to be dismissed. He was not meek and she knew it, there was a reason he had braved the storm outside and somehow she doubted it was to check on her family.

Mark must have felt the same way since no offer of anything escaped his lips and Mr. Fulton went on to more pressing matters. "Did your pipes freeze?" Arthur Fulton asked standing at the top of the stairs, looking no warmer than he had when he stepped through the front door. Maybe he had expected them to have a fire burning and electricity blazing overhead. Mark was good, but not that good.

"No," Mark replied. "We filled the bathtub to empty the pipes". Mr. Fulton gave an incredulous nod as if disappointed he had not thought of that idea all the while his head turned this way and that and his eyes darted everywhere, never meeting Mark's, as if he were only half listening while he cased the joint.

He started to walk down the hall away from Mark and Regan. Looking at Mark, Regan raised her eyebrows as if to say go after him. Mark begrudgingly obliged, breaking into a little jog to catch up to the old man. It didn't take much as he hadn't gone too far. Regan was starting to wonder how on earth he had made it across the street, but more importantly, would he make it back? She knew that at the first sign of trouble her husband would risk his own safety to help the old man get home.

"No broken windows? Or drafts?" Mr. Fulton continued to press. "None," Mark beamed. "I winterized the house last fall so she is sealed up tight." Mark had insisted on sealing every draft in an effort to keep them more comfortable because the year before, the front door had seemed to warp and when you held a hand up to any of the seams cold air spilled inside.

"Hmm," was all he said in response, "And your tree doesn't seem to be a problem," he stated not mentioning his maple that was now horizontal in the front yard sticking out of a transformer. "I saw the twins last night. It looked like they were bringing their Barbecue into the kitchen." The twins he referred to were Norma and Nina Fitzpatrick, two lovely ladies in their sixties that had lived together all their lives, neither one of them having been married. They had the pleasure of living next door to Arthur Fulton. Whenever Regan had seen the sisters they would wave and come over with some kind of sweet for the kids. So of course Ainslie and Josh adored them. Last summer Josh had even helped them do some gardening and struck a deal to shovel their driveway this year.

"Oh dear," Regan said. "That isn't smart," said Mark. "They might start a fire or end up filling the house with smoke if they are cooking on it." He scowled, "People are cold and will do whatever it takes to get warm." Arthur stated, with no emotion in his voice whatsoever. It was as if he didn't care about anyone on the street, but he cared about the street itself. He then started to fidget with a pull in his sweater. Regan got the distinct impression that he wanted to ask something but couldn't bring himself to. He gave the impression that he was a proud man.

"Well, I guess I better get home. You seem alright over here. Do you mind if I use the bathroom? It is a long way back in this weather, took me a good fifteen minutes to get here from across the street," Mark was taken aback by the request. In this situation you would expect a request for food or water, after all you can do your business out a window if need be.

"Um, okay," Mark pointed to the main bathroom and Mr. Fulton disappeared.

Regan came down the hall to meet her husband. "What do you think he wants?" she whispered. Mark just shrugged and then they heard it. Water, it was the glug, glug, sound of a bottle being filled in the bathtub.

Regan ran down the hall and knocked on the door. "Just a minute," Mr. Fulton called. "Arthur open the door now," Regan demanded. Mark had disappeared. "Almost done," he replied as sweetly as he could.

She knocked again. This time there was no answer. She felt Mark's presence behind her and the very distinguishable clunk clunk of a shot gun being primed.

"Arthur," he called. "Do you know what that sound was? I am loading my shotgun Arthur so open the fucking door," he snarled quietly through the bathroom door so the kids would not hear.

Mr. Fulton opened the door with his hands in the air. "I'm not doing anything," he claimed. They could see water on the floor beside the tub. The old man followed their gaze looking very guilty. And his pants were wet on the outside of the leg.

Mark grabbed him roughly by the front of his sweater with his free hand and yanked him out of the bathroom. He almost flew through the air from the force. There was not much to him. And for a moment Regan panicked thinking the aggression that Mark was using might end in a broken bone or heart attack as the man had gone a deathly white. She knew the shotgun was just posturing and knew that Mark had no intention of killing anyone while at the same time he had a crazed look in his eye and she did not want to test that theory right now.

The water was still rippling from whatever had been in it. Mark went into the small room to see if anything was out of place. He couldn't tell, but he knew the old man had been up to something.

"What did you do?" Mark demanded, the shotgun temporarily forgotten pointed at the floor from his right hand, its flat black finish looking menacing. "Did you put something in it?" Mark's voice started to rise. "What did you do?"

Mr. Fulton still had his hands up, and had lost all of his threatening demeanor, he just looked like a sad, weak old man now. From behind he had a very noticeable hump. It was almost comical to behold. Did he think they wouldn't notice that there was something stuffed under his sweater? A hysterical laugh escaped Regan and she pointed at Mr. Fulton's back.

Mark spun him around. "Ah Jesus Arthur," Mark exclaimed yanking the back of the old man's sweater up with one hand to reveal what he was hiding. The man looked his age, the sunken cheeks, the sinewy hands still held in the air, even his clothes made him seem old. His head drooped from disappointing his only friend, he knew he was caught and there would be no repairing this rift with Mark.

It turned out he had hidden a collapsible plastic camping jug under his clothes. He was using it to steal some water from them and now he was caught. He had known that Mark had an interest in survival and had come for the water he so critically needed. How he had expected to sneak out of the house with that was anyone's guess.

"I'm desperate. Not much food, no water, and the house is freezing," he explained trying to look sorry and pitiful at the same time. "You could have asked," was Mark's angry response. "But now you steal from my family! I have kids for god's sake Arthur. I would have given you whatever you needed if you had just asked."

Mr. Fulton turned to Regan for sympathy, but did not find it. With his mouth open, there were no words to explain this away. "Get out!" She said firmly. "You can take the bottle, but don't come back here again."

The old man was flustered and tried to quickly put on everything that he had taken off upon entering the house. Looking around for his gloves that he had forgotten he put in his pocket. Then sheepishly he said to both Mark and Regan, "I'm sorry." And Mark replied, "yeah, so am I." and with that, he yanked the door open and let in a gale of cold wind, then the old man was gone. Mark slammed the door behind him, stepping through the remaining little pile of snow. He cursed and sat on the bottom step removing his now wet socks throwing them in the corner of the floor.

"Wow," Regan said to her husband. "I hope the power comes back on soon, for his sake." Mark didn't reply. He went into the kitchen and placed the shotgun in one of the lower cabinets, locking it up and putting the key in his pant pocket. Regan didn't like that he hadn't put the gun back in the gun safe that was occupying space in their walk-in closet. She also noted that it had been loaded. Was he expecting more trouble? She appeased herself with the old adage, "its' better to be safe than sorry." He went down the hall to their bedroom and returned with a fresh pair of dry socks.

Surprisingly, the kids didn't bombard them with questions about their neighbour or the fact that Mark had taken out the shotgun. In time Regan knew the questions would come, but for now they just sat quietly sensing the tension and their father's anger with the strange little old man that had just left their house.

The rest of the afternoon passed much the same as the one before. Trying to keep the kids occupied with games and stories and an occasional update from the radio. At one point, Regan and Josh put on their coats, hats, two pairs of gloves, snow pants and boots to go out the basement door to shovel the landing for Caesar and Scamp. The door sat below ground level at the foot of five steps that lead to the lawn above somewhat protecting the door from the wind and the overhang of roof helped prevent a buildup of snow. Regan knew she would have to disinfect the stairs leading up to the yard after this, but for now the dogs would have a safe place to relieve themselves and that was more important right now.

When they came back in the house Regan told her son to go upstairs and take all of his outdoor clothes off and leave them at the front door then change any piece of clothing that was wet. When he was gone Regan stood in the basement gloom and exhaled. She could see her breath mist as she watched it. "That's not good," she thought to herself. The temperature was dropping in the house. If the heat didn't come on soon they would have to figure out a better way to keep warm than just piling on layers of clothing and blankets. Her thoughts turned to the twins and their barbeque. They were either toasty warm, or passed out from smoke inhalation. Maybe it wasn't such a bad idea, maybe they were on to something and they should follow that lead. But Regan knew better, it was just the cold talking.

*Keeping a spare propane cylinder is always a good idea. In the cold, it gives you a few options to keep warm before there's a need to dig a fire pit. Never take your BBQ into the house, I cannot stress this enough. You can set the house on fire, or fill it with smoke. – Survival Tips for the Urban Idiot*

The windows had frosted over on the inside through the night so Regan went to the kitchen and retrieved a couple of butter knives and her and Mark used them to chip away at the ice while being careful not to touch their skin to it. The sky was black and they had slept in as a result thinking it was still early. The lighting had thrown them off as it was almost nine o'clock and they were not seeing any sign of daylight. Could it be storm clouds making the sky seem so dark? The back windows seemed to have more light streaming through, giving the illusion of a black cloud hanging over Sunset Place.

"Oh my god," Regan gasped as Mark managed to clear

55

the glass enough to see out. He then stood staring in awe at the scene before him. The twin's house must have caught on fire at some point the night before, leaving just a smoking crater where the two-story once stood. "They brought their barbeque into the house," Mark murmured, recalling what Mr. Fulton had told them.

They both stood there for a while trying not to think about the fate of the two kindly old ladies, but knowing that even if the twins had gotten out of the house they would probably not have been strong enough to get through all of the icy snow. Norma had a bad heart and her sister had undergone hip surgery the month before, making it virtually impossible for them to have escaped.

The snow had melted around the burned out house creating a bowl effect, but you could still see how deep it would have been for their escape. The black tipped drifts were almost as high as where the second story would have started had it still been there.

Regan was covered in goosebumps as Mark slid his arm up to her shoulders, and pulled her to him. She was saddened by the scene, but thankful that her own family was still okay, which made her feel guilty. With each passing day it was feeling more and more like rescue was not coming.

Breaking away from his embrace she had an urge to stick to her new daily routine. She headed for the light switch as she had every day, desperately hoping that today would be the day they turned on. But as was the case for the past 3 days, nothing happened. The house was bitterly cold this morning and sleet had started to fall, "just what we need, more ice." She muttered to herself. It didn't seem to be melting the snow, but fortifying it by creating an impenetrable outer shell leaving the snow as strong as concrete.

The house was gloomy, the haze from the smoke outside mixed with the emotions of the two adults inside did not make for a potentially good day. Regan was going to be short with everyone and Mark was worried about his wife. He needed to do something to bring her around, she couldn't give up, and it seemed that she was on the brink of doing just that.

"Hey guys," he whispered loudly to the kids as they woke up, waving them into the kitchen. Once they were all assembled in the kitchen out of Regan's earshot, he turned to them and said, "Why don't we make breakfast for mommy this morning?" Ainslie perked up, "Like we do for mother's day?" she asked excitedly. "Exactly like that," Mark said. "Sure," Josh replied yawning. Ainslie did a quick footed little jig holding onto her bunny that she had slept with. Mark took that to mean that she consented.

Regan had gone back to the fort and yanked the canopy off the top so that she could see out the window while lying on the floor. "How much longer would this last?" She wondered to herself. These past three days had felt more like 3 weeks. The need to call her boss had left her. After all, he couldn't fire her for not contacting him when there was no way to do it. Lifting her arm up to shield her eyes, she felt like crying. But what was the point of that? She bit the inside of her cheek to stop the flow of tears from coming. That would just upset the kids. She needed to be strong for them and Mark too. They were in this together.

In the kitchen, Mark and the kids were collecting ingredients for a make-shift breakfast in bed. There were only two pieces of bread left, so they put them back and found some eggs, flour and what was left of the milk and mixed it up in a bowl. Then using a cookie sheet and the little cast iron rings normally used for poached eggs they poured in the batter creating six decent sized soon to be pancakes.

The radio stood on the counter and Mark, hoping for an update, turned it on. He was met with static. He quickly tried to turn it off, but it was too late. "What was that?" Regan inquired from the living room. Mark was trying to come up with something that would not send his wife's day into a further downward spiral when Ainslie blurted out, "radio's not working!" Mark just slumped his shoulders and resided himself to the fact that she was going to find out sooner or later. There was no reply from Regan.

Mark then donned his outdoor gear and braced himself for the elements he was about to face to get to the barbecue on the deck.

After a little bit of rocking the sliding door back and forth, it finally gave in and he was able to get out on the deck. The barbecue was a little different. He had to yank the cast iron beast out of a frozen drift that had collected around it and partially dragging partially rolling it on its wheels he positioned it just outside the slider door, taking note that in the winter this might be its permanent place in the event that this ever happened again, they would have easy access to it. Mark then sparked it up, hoping against hope that it did not have any frozen lines preventing it from working. Mark heard the gas hissing and gave a jump for joy when he heard the whoosh of the igniter catching. He closed the lid and headed back into the house. The sleet was still falling, and it chilled to the bone, but they all needed this.

"What are you doing?" Regan asked from the floor not moving her arm from her eyes. "It's a surprise," Mark whispered loudly so she could hear him. "Okay," she whispered back in a mocking tone unable to hide a smile from underneath her arm.

Josh appeared with the cookie sheet, ready to help his dad. Mark motioned for him to put it down on the dining room table. Mark didn't take off his exterior clothes; he just waited and watched the barbeque, praying that it didn't go out. When the remaining snow started to disappear, sliding down the lid in its liquid form, Mark took the tray and headed back outside. He was trying to be quick so that he could retain whatever heat was left in the house. The wind was not as bad today, but the dampness from the sleet cut straight through to the bone.

Out on the deck he walked carefully to make sure he didn't slip on the gathering frost under his feet. He then placed the cookie sheet on the upper grill of the barbecue and closed the lid again. He was excited by the prospect of some warm food in his belly. It had been days of cold food, and every time he ate something, the desire for a steak, or some spaghetti, or even a warm cup of coffee returned to him, each time more intense than the last. Now that the barbecue was functional and the fridge was almost empty, they would have to use it more, starting in on their canned goods inventory.

He slipped into the house again. There seemed to be very little difference between the temperature outside and inside the house. Layering was one thing, but they needed a warming source. He wished that he had invested in a wood stove when Kevin-Regan's father-had bought his house and it came with one. It definitely would've come in handy right about now.

That gave him a great idea! Something they used to do on camping trips when he was a kid and it got cold at night. This past summer he had thought about making a fire pit in the backyard. Although he hadn't dug the pit he had purchased the stones to edge it with, and luckily, he had been too lazy to put them in the shed like Regan had been nagging him to do, so they were piled at the corner of the deck. "Ha, take that Regan! Score one for your bum of a husband."

He went back out and checked the pancakes, quickly flipping them, and then he went to find the stones. His footing was getting treacherous out on the deck so he was choosing each step carefully. He found them buried in the snow on the corner of the deck. He then put one of them on the lower rack of the barbeque to warm up. He could only fit one at a time because of their size, but if he hadn't been making the pancakes he could have warmed two at once.

By now, the pancakes were looking pretty done so he brought them inside and called to Josh and Ainslie. Both kids appeared, one with plates the other with maple syrup and cutlery. Mark quickly put the pancakes onto a plate and handed it to Ainslie. "What is that wonderful smell?" Regan asked, turning towards them. "Pancakes," Ainslie shouted while running towards her mother with a plate full of them. "I've got the syrup," Josh called after her. Sitting up, Regan was all smiles and held up her hands to slow her daughter down, although at this point it wouldn't matter if those hot little cakes fell on the floor. She was sure they all would have eaten them regardless, unless Caesar or Scamp beat them to it.

Mark slipped back out to the stones and threw another

one on the barbeque, then went back inside to have a pancake with his family. Once again, he didn't remove his outer things, just sat at the dining room table. Josh brought him a pancake and it was the best thing he had ever eaten. His son sat down beside him at the dining table and asked, "Are you making more?" Mark looked up, "Do you want more?" Josh nodded, and Mark said, "Okay go pour some more out on the tray like we did before. Can you do that?" Josh nodded emphatically. "I have something else on the barbecue but it should be just about ready." Josh gave him a queer look as he had only been involved in the pancake prep. Surprisingly, he didn't question his father, disappearing back into the kitchen to whip up another batch of batter for the barbeque.

Mark headed back outside while he pulled his waterproof mittens on tight, then he grabbed the stone. He could feel the heat through the material protecting his hands, but the gloves were thick enough so he would not be burned. Steam rose from the stone every time the icy sleet made contact and Mark knew he had to hurry.

He managed to hold the stone in one hand while he opened the slider with the other. He entered the house and called to Ainslie. "Can you please bring me one of the sheets from the fort?" She grabbed one of the flannel linens and brought it to her father. He wrapped the sheet around the stone and placed it on the floor. Before he went outside again he asked her to bring another sheet and leave it by the door for him. Josh appeared with the tray of pancake batter and Mark took it with him back outside. He put the tray on the top rack and removed the other stone, taking it into the house and wrapping it in the other sheet. He had time to warm two more stones while the pancakes browned.

Ten minutes later, they were all sitting on the floor surrounded by warm stones and eating pancakes. The kids were chattering excitedly at having been a part of making breakfast and getting to help their dad. Regan seemed in better spirits as the cold had abated for the time being in their little area. It seemed like what they all needed was something to do. Could that have been all that was missing? Mark started to think about what they could do in the afternoon. Once those stones cooled they would need to be put back outside because just as they had held the heat they would cling to the cold. The kids could help with that, they would just need to be careful and take their time; he didn't need any squashed feet or serious injuries. The moving around would help keep them warm too. Mark couldn't stop smiling.

After the horrible start to the day, Regan was relieved to have something seem to go right. She had been concerned she was slipping into a depression. That kind of emotional reaction seemed inevitable, but would serve no purpose in this situation, she knew that and vowed to herself to keep a better grip on her emotions which might prove harder than she thought.  Even as she was thinking about it, she couldn't help but feel anxiety creep in. "We are all restless, the kids don't know what to do with themselves, water and food feel like they are running low since no end is in site and how much propane is in that tank?" Regan smiled all the same so that her family wouldn't see the worry that was disconcerting her. The charred remains of the house across the street were at her back. She could feel them looming there as if someone were standing behind her, breathing on her neck.

Mark looked at Regan. She was smiling at them all, but he had known her for a long time and he could see that smile was for their benefit. She kept on looking over her shoulder, checking the street in her peripheral vision as if the house that had burned down would somehow be standing just as it had the day before. The thought of her in pain made him sad. He could never bear to see her upset always going out of his way to cheer her up when she was down. He wasn't sure where that came from but his mother had battled with depression for years, attempting suicide twice. It must be his way of trying to prevent Regan from becoming depressed. Logically he knew that was impossible, depression was a mental health issue and it didn't matter if he could make her laugh constantly it would return, a truth he learned in his youth. But what was occurring had nothing to do with depression. Two ladies had died on their street. Ladies that Regan and Mark both knew and liked. He felt guilty at the thought of sleeping soundly while the two ladies had tried to fight for their lives. Horrible visions came to mind of fire and gore.

Mark gave his head a shake, and started to clear up the dishes. As he stood up, he kissed Regan on her forehead. She closed her eyes and leaned into it. "Thank you," she said, opening her eyes. She looked so beautiful staring up at him with her pale blue eyes, her ash blond hair falling away from her face. He was reminded of when they were dating and the same feeling came over him. He smiled down at her and gently brushed the knuckle of his left hand across her cheek wiping away a tear that was not there.

"Come on rugrats," he called to the kids. "Let's go take care of some business." Josh and Ainslie jumped up to follow their dad into the kitchen carrying the maple syrup and paper napkins they had used during their feast. A few minutes later Ainslie appeared running to the pile of blankets where they had slept and lifted her pillow into the air. "Aww," she complained loudly. "She never came." In her hand she held up the little tooth that she had lost the day before. "Oh Jesus," Regan had forgotten. Ainslie was pouting and Regan said to her, "the weather is pretty bad. It would be hard to fly in this. I'm sure once the snow stops we can try again and she will come." Ainslie still held her tooth in the air possibly trying to come up with a plan to cash in on the piece of bone when Caesar came along and with one lick he snatched the tooth and crunched it in his mouth. "No!" she yelled at the dog. "Caesar you are a bad boy!" And with that she swatted him on the nose. The big dog cowered, backing away from the tiny girl. "Ainslie, don't do that to him," Regan scolded. "He ate my tooth," she whined. "He doesn't know any better." Regan tried to soothe her daughter. "Why don't we write a letter and explain to the tooth fairy what happened. I'm sure she will understand." Ainslie stood for a minute with her bottom lip sticking out; arms folded looking at the dog that had just taken her treasure. And just like that she let her arms go and said, "Will you help me write it mommy?" Regan nodded her head and Ainslie headed back toward the kitchen to tell her dad and brother what had just happened.

After her daughter left Regan pulled the blanket up around her and dared a peak at the house across the street only turning her head, not committing her whole body to the torture. The smoke had subsided and was no more then what you would see at a campfire. It freaked her out to see the blackened remains. "Please, let it snow some more," she silently prayed to herself not really wanting more snow, but hoping to create an out of sight, out of mind scenario, with the snow forming a blanket to hide the horrors of the night before.

She could hear Mark talking to the kids in the kitchen, but wasn't really listening to what he was saying. From the tone of his voice, it sounded like he was doling out jobs for them to do. Regan stood up and stretched her arms above her head letting the blanket slide to the floor and looked around at the disaster the living room had become. She started to organize the area; having pulled off the canopy, it could no longer be called a tent or a fort. She folded the king-size blanket and placed it on the couch. Then, she busied herself with piling up the pillows and straightening the bedding that was still lying on the floor. Scamp's squeaky toy was buried beneath some of the covers and when she threw the newspaper shaped toy to the other side of the room (the daily growl). He appeared as if from nowhere and tore after the toy. The last items that were out of place were the kid's slippers and Ainslie's basketball net that had served as the main support for the overhead blanket. The footwear was askew so Regan gave them a little place at the end of the couch, lining them up ready to be worn. And she carried the little basketball net down the hall back to Ainslie's room then returned the way she had come, and stood in the living room. She surveyed her work. "Well," she pondered. "It is better than it was a few minutes ago." How could she possibly clean up a room that had blankets and pillows lying on the floor, the couch and chairs all out of place and clothes and slippers everywhere? Not to mention dog toys, although the toys were always lying around. Mark had tried to train both canines to put their toys away in a basket that still sat in the living room, but Regan hadn't enforced the rule and in the end Mark got frustrated       and         gave         up.

*When keeping warm, there are the obvious things you can do, like listen to your mom and wear a jacket. One word people, LAYERS! For those of you who have grown up in winter wonderlands you are familiar with this way of thinking. For those of you who didn't, well, layering is a time honored tradition constantly utilized in frozen wastelands. —Survival Tips for the Urban Idiot*

Regan couldn't help but look out the window. The wind and sleet were casting a gray shadow on the day giving the blackened crater an even more menacing look.

The last time she had seen the two old biddies came drifting back to her. Norma would religiously take her twin out for a daily walk, even if it was just up and down the driveway to make sure her hip didn't stiffen up. Regan had waved to them while driving past on her way to the grocery store just this past Saturday and they had waved in response.

"They took their barbeque into the house," Mr. Fulton's words came back to her. "Why didn't he warn them?" She asked herself. "I could have gone over to help them," but she knew that just wasn't true, the risk was too great otherwise they would be going up and down the street to help whoever needed it. She felt helpless and pathetic. Not to mention her anxiety seemed to be returning, the sensation of numbness that always occurred on the right side of her throat creating the feeling that she couldn't swallow and had to really think about the task every time it needed to be completed. The tingling in her arms not quite the same as when a limb fell asleep but close enough, and the worst of all was the restless buzzing that seemed to come from somewhere in the core of her being. The overwhelming urge to do something, but not wanting to move, it was like drinking ten cups of coffee, chasing them with a Red bull and all you can do is ride it out. She ran both her flexed hands down the front of her pants and shook her upper body, as if she was trying to work out some excess energy. She rubbed her fingers against the palms of her hands until the sensation subsided. Sometimes it went away immediately and sometimes it stuck around, recurring throughout the day. She had the feeling that it would be back throughout the day today; experience told her distraction would help. She found herself looking out the window again.

Mark had the kids lined up in the kitchen like a little assembly line. First, Josh had gotten a bowl of water from the bathtub and Ainslie had put the plug in the sink. While Josh poured the water in, Ainslie squirted the dish soap. Then Mark washed the dishes by hand. He handed them off to Josh beside him who would then dry them and handed them to Ainslie who sat on the counter and put them away. Next, they were preparing lunch. The whole wheat bread was piled high on one of the paper plates and Josh was buttering each slice, then passing them to Ainslie, who put a handful of mini carrots on a plate with two slices of buttered bread then slid them to their dad who then cut the corned beef into slices and placed it on the bread building the sandwich and cutting it in half. The plan was to help Regan out as much as they could today and the kids were more than willing to.

Once the sandwiches were all assembled, they carted the feast out to Regan who was still in the living room by herself. "Woah," exclaimed Mark. "Mommy cleaned up for us." He smirked at Regan. She dropped her shoulders and fanned her hands out as if presenting some wonderful prize on a game show.

He handed her a plate and they sat down on the couch. Ainslie and Josh sat on the floor and went to town eating their lunch; they had worked up an appetite. Caesar stayed close by just in case a morsel got away from the kids, a tooth wasn't enough to fill his large belly. Five second rule or not, he was claiming it.

Quiet fell over the room as they all ate their meal. Nobody felt the need to fill the silence. The truth was, they were all starting to get used to the quiet. It was enjoyable at times, but on a day like today it was all Regan could do not to scream at the top of her lungs. She had purposefully turned her back on the front window and angled her body towards her husband sitting next to her so she could look at him while she ate and not have any view of the street.

Ainslie made a high pitched squeak that cut off abruptly, her hands instinctually going to her neck. Regan, Mark and Josh all turned to look at her, she had stood up and panic painted her face. She was trying to cough, her mouth open, her tongue sticking out slightly, but no noise was coming out. Regan stood up, "Ainslie are you choking?" She reached out to her daughter and Ainslie's dark red face was the only answer she needed. The little girl was jumping up and down now thumping her hand against her chest. Regan grabbed her around her tiny waist and drove her clasped fists up under the little girl's ribcage, lifting her off the ground. Regan put her back on the ground. Mark, who was in front of his daughter, shouted, "do it again!" to his wife. Regan drove her fists into the little girl's abdomen again. She could feel her little girl losing strength and going a little slack as she held her. Regan gave it all she had and lifted the girl into the air one more time. There was a popping noise as something flew across the room out of the girl's mouth. Caesar ran after it and caught it mid-air, licking his lips. Ainslie made a sucking sound as she gasped in air. Regan cradled her daughter in her arms and asked if she was okay. Ainslie reached for her mother and started to cry. Josh had been sitting frozen watching the ordeal. He put his sandwich down gently onto the plate lying on the floor. Nothing like seeing your sibling almost die to make you lose your appetite.

Regan was shaking and holding Ainslie close. Mark came over and hugged them both, sitting on the ground and leaving a comforting hand on Ainslie's back. Even though this was an incident that could have happened in a normal setting, on a sunny day with the power on, the point that they were on their own hit home once again.

Josh appeared with Ainslie's bunny and handed the rabbit to his sister. She took it and hugged the animal close. They stayed that way for a little while, thankful that they were all still in one piece.

Ainslie would not leave her mother's side all afternoon. Even when she went to the washroom, when Regan opened the door, the little girl was sitting there waiting. Regan couldn't help but smile. She had saved her daughter. When the shit hit the fan, she was calm and able to act. That had been a fear all her life; the possibility that she would freeze in a crisis situation. She had once considered becoming a nurse, a doctor was never an option as her grades were okay but not great. A nurse though would help her satisfy her want to help people and she wasn't squeamish, but the thought of working shifts and possibly weekends would have been too difficult to coordinate with Mark and the kids so she had put that aside for her rewarding career in customer service!

Regan told Ainslie to get some crayons and paper from her room, they were going to write a letter to the tooth fairy. That made her daughter very happy. Josh seemed a little bored, so Regan asked if he would like to write a letter to anyone or draw something. He just shrugged and didn't really answer.

When Ainslie appeared, Regan gave her the little laptop tray her father used when he worked in the living room. It helped to keep his laptop from heating up and right now it provided his daughter with a flat surface to write her letter on. Ainslie chose a pink crayon to start her letter with and changed the color with each new word she wrote, giving the letter a rainbow look. She knew exactly what she wanted to say and got to work. Josh took a fine tipped Sharpie and started to draw. Regan sat with her back against the couch and wondered where Mark had gone. He disappeared from the living room at some point and wherever he was, he was being very quiet because she couldn't detect any noises with her super-sonic mom hearing.

Mark had slipped into the master bedroom shortly after the dust had settled from Ainslie's choking incident. He sat on the bed and tears rushed to his eyes spilling down his cheeks. He sobbed quietly with his hand over his mouth. The look of horror on his daughter's face stuck in his brain as if it was tattooed on the back of his eye lids. He lay down on the bed and curled up into the fetal position, feeling disappointed that he had not been the one to act, and shaken by the vulnerability of their situation. He cried himself to sleep.

Time slipped by and the kids kept on drawing and writing letters. Josh had drawn some cool action pictures of Manga style characters. He was an excellent artist; Regan assumed that came from Mark's side of the family as she had trouble drawing a stick figure. Then the two kids had started writing letters to each other and making the little notes into paper airplanes, sailing them across the room to one another, littering the living room floor with the flimsy aircrafts. Regan let them have their fun. Ainslie had finished her tooth fairy letter that she then proceeded to cover in sparkles, which ended up all over everything. Regan picked up the letter and read it to herself:

Dear TF, (love the fact she has given the tooth fairy a nickname)

How are you? I am okay. I wish it would stop snowing . I miss recess. Mommy won't let us go outside cos of the storm. Cezer ate my tooth that is why its gone. Can I still have a new toothbrush?

Love,

Ainslie Peyton Davis

Regan smiled. The little girl had asked when to use her middle name not that long ago and Regan had responded with, "whenever you want." So from that point on Ainslie had used her full name and initials as often as possible.

Mark came walking down the hall, his eyes glossy with sleep. He gave Regan a half-hearted wave as he turned into the kitchen. She looked at him quizzically before getting up to join him. "Where were you?" She asked once she caught up. He looked down at his wife and sighed deeply. "I needed a minute," he responded in a monotone voice. She furrowed her brow and asked, "everything okay?" He nodded, and said again, "I just needed a minute." It dawned on Regan what he meant. "She's okay," meaning Ainslie. "She even seems to be over the shock of it," Regan tried to console him. He turned away from her to gaze out the window. "I froze," he said to her. Regan put a reassuring hand on his shoulder, "only because I stepped in. Come on Mark do you really think that you would have been able to sit there and do nothing if I hadn't given her the Heimlich?" Mark stood quietly thinking for a moment and then said, "no." Regan smiled and said, "Exactly, I know you wouldn't. If I didn't act you would have. It's always been that way with us. Do you remember when I slammed Josh's little fingers in the van door when he was two?" He nodded, "how could I forget," he murmured. Josh was so little and his tiny fingers were disfigured from the force of the car door. "I couldn't even think to open the door but you got him out strapped him in his car seat used the ice from the drink you had to keep the swelling down and got him to the hospital for help." The last thing she said hung between them like some heavy object over their heads threatening to fall and crush them; they were both trying to ignore it but knew it was there. If something were to happen, the hospital was not an option right now.

"If you want some time you can go lie down in the room. I think it might do you some good to have a little escape," Mark offered. Regan shook her head, "I'm okay right now." The last thing she wanted was to be alone with her thoughts; she turned away from him and headed back out to the living room.

The kids had made Caesar a paper hat and the patient dog was lying obediently wearing it. Regan burst out laughing when she saw him. The poor pup looked so ridiculous in his head wear. Mark came to see what was so funny and lost it, guffawing at the poor animal's expense. Caesar looked at them with his big sad eyes.

The light outside was starting to fade and Regan told the kids to start picking up all of the paper and put the crayons and markers away. They didn't even try to argue with her. "So it is technology that's the problem after all, good to know!" She thought to herself, referring to the resistance she usually got if they were watching a show or playing a video game.

With the light fading they would have to get a move on with dinner and warming the stones. Regan went back into the kitchen to see what they had left in the canned goods inventory.

Ten minutes later, two tins of pasta and one stone were warming up on the barbeque. Mark had braved the elements and was standing at the back door watching the cast iron oven struggle to maintain its heat. He knew that one of these days he would be met with no propane left in the tank, but there was a spare in the garage. He hoped he wouldn't have to go get it though, as they hadn't been out in that little area of the backyard where the side door to the house and the pathway to the garage door were. It was possible that they wouldn't be able to access it. They were okay for now though. He was pretty sure that he had filled the tank just before the summer had ended. That was usually a getting ready for fall item on the "to do list".

Regan appeared with an arm full of clothes once again. She didn't have to explain, he knew she was having the kids add more layers to keep warm. They didn't seem to like sleeping with socks or gloves on, but that was where they were most vulnerable. He smiled at Regan. She was a good mother, and he was so proud of her for that. It was always the kids first in her mind. "You could use some too," he called across the room to her. She started at the sound of his voice, not paying him any attention when she walked in. "What?" She asked looking at him now. "I said you could use some too," he replied pointing to the pile she had just laid down on the couch. A smile spread across her face, "I'm okay." And with that she turned on her heal and disappeared again. Mark went outside to check on their meal.

The stones were setup and warming the room, dinner was served, and everyone was bundled up for the night before even the first stars were dotting the sky.

Mark opened the drapes all the way so that they could all see out the big front window; the frost had melted throughout the day and provided a clear view out of the glass. The night was calm and the constellations could be seen clear as day. Regan quickly used the only astrological knowledge she had, "there's Orion's belt." The three stars in a row shone in the night sky. "Who's Orion?" Josh asked. Regan sheepishly admitted, "I don't really know." It didn't seem to matter that Regan and Mark couldn't name all of the constellations or even individual stars, the children were amazed by the beauty of the night sky and marveled at it for some time. The moon was full and Josh said, "werewolves come out when there's a full moon." Mark and Regan saw the look on Ainslie's face, and then shared a sideways glance before Mark said sternly, "There are no such things as werewolves Josh." And that was the end of the star gazing.

Everyone got settled into the make-shift bed on the floor. Regan gathered all of the dishes and took them into the kitchen to throw them in the trash. She saw her phone on the counter and turned it on to see if she had any messages, there was nothing. "Come on mom!" Josh shouted from the living room, so she set it back down on the counter and headed to the living room to set about reading from their book.

They were almost finished the first Harry Potter book, but Regan knew there were seven books in the series. Her stomach tightened at the thought of actually finishing the series during the blackout. "Was it possible for the power to be off for that long?" She wondered to herself. She forced the though away. "You are overreacting. It has only been a couple of days, won't be much longer," she tried to reassure herself.

Caesar chose that moment to howl, startling the family. "WEREWOLF!" Ainslie screamed and threw the covers over her head. Josh was pale and shaken. The mythical monsters must have been on both of their minds after seeing the full moon. Regan put her arms around her shaking children and pulled them close to her. "It's just Caesar," Mark said. "Come here boy," he called to the dog and Scamp as well as Caesar charged at him knocking him over. The sight of their father being stampeded by the dogs made the kids laugh. Caesar went over to Ainslie and put his head on the ground in front of her. She patted his huge head and whispered that he was a good dog, but the howling scared her and would he mind not doing that again until the lights came back on? Caesar just kept looking up at her from where his head rested on the floor. "Can we get back to the story now?" Regan asked.

She read for a little while longer. It seemed to take longer for everybody to settle down and fall asleep that night. Caesar stayed by Ainslie all night, her tiny hand resting on his head for comfort.

Regan put the book quietly down when she was sure the kids were asleep. She flipped from her back to her stomach and looked at her sleeping family. She was actually feeling tired and content tonight. She closed her eyes and was asleep almost immediately, falling into a fitful kind of unconscious. Haunted by nonsensical images that she could not make out.

# 8 DAY FOUR - MORNING

*You are not always with your family so for the people that you care about establish a designated meeting place. Stay calm and find the best way to get to this place, but don't risk your well-being to get there. If a storm is raging outside, stay put. Once the weather clears, then you can make your way to this meeting place, just ensure everyone knows the plan. If you are outside when calamity strikes, seek shelter immediately. – Survival Tips for the Urban Idiot*

Regan's phone was buzzing from the kitchen counter. She heard it immediately and her eyes flew open at the sound. Swiftly and silently, she slipped out of the blankets and made her way to the kitchen, wiping the sleep out of her eyes and yawning as she went. She snatched the device from the counter before it could make any more noise. It was probably a text message from Sam. She stood in the kitchen holding the device and all she could think of was why had her phone been left on?!

The little red light in the upper left hand corner of the phone let her know that there was a message waiting for her. She swiped the screen to open the message. Sam's face smiled up at her from the phone; it was her Facebook picture. It looked like it had been taken in her backyard during the summer. Her chestnut hair was pulled back in a ponytail, a blue t-shirt enhancing her blue eyes. She looked a little tanned as well. In the picture she was holding up some kind of tropical looking drink garnished with pineapple in a cheers motion for the camera. "Oh, summer," Regan thought to herself. She almost couldn't remember how it felt to feel the sun warming her skin and was starting to wonder if she ever would again.

She touched the picture of her sister and the message appeared. It said, "How are you guys doing? Heard from mom and dad, they are okay. Dad dropped some of the logs he was bringing into the house for the wood stove on his foot and broke it. He has been to the hospital, don't worry. It was a clean break apparently, so they just set it and hooked him up with a cast and some crutches. They also have their power back on, so there's really no need to worry about them, just focus on keeping yourself and the family warm and as comfortable as possible."

Regan stared at the message for a long time in disbelief. It was surreal to imagine that the whole world was not at a standstill. Her parents had power and were safe; she glanced at the stove clock to make sure it was still dark, it was. She almost resented them, "we live in the suburbs shouldn't those areas be up and running before the rural areas?" she asked herself. Why wasn't she happy that her parents were safe? How could she be so selfish? She didn't normally consider herself a selfish person, but maybe she was wrong. Her own discomfort was getting in the way of being happy her parents were okay. She was relieved, just not happy.

She responded to her sister with, "that's great! Ours is still out, but hoping that may be a sign this will end soon.

Phone's dying gotta go." With that she turned the phone off and placed it back on the counter where she had picked it up. She went to the kitchen window and looked out. The snow had stopped, the wind seemed to have settled down, but it was still cloudy as if the frozen precipitation could start again at any minute. Regan turned to go back to the living room when the clouds broke and she could feel the warmth of the sun on her back. She turned back to the little window and had to squint at the light coming in. Closing her eyes, she enjoyed the moment as that was all it was. Seconds passed and she could feel the sun disappear behind some of the clouds and the cold return. She opened her eyes, wondering if she had just imagined it. Real or imagined, it gave her hope. She felt a little more positive today, that had to have something to do with knowing that her parents were safe, didn't it? It could be worse she pondered, "There could be zombies, a plague or some other apocalyptic event that they had to deal with and in that case there would never be an end in sight," Wow, too much television.

Eyeing the little radio, she thought, "What the hell," and clicked the switch to on. Only static came out of the little speakers so she snapped the switch back to the off position. Still nothing.

She headed out of the kitchen and surveyed her family still lying on the floor. Stopping at the light switch, she couldn't help but check, even though she was pretty certain that nothing was going to happen. She flicked it up and nothing happened so she flicked the switch back down. Mark was awake and fidgeting with the blanket that covered him. Ainslie was asleep; lying with her head on Caesar's back, rising and falling with each breath he took. Josh was sprawled all over the floor, still sound asleep. Regan wondered which one of them had used her phone and left it on. The initial anger at such a thoughtless act came back to her, so she decided to use the process of elimination and went to the only other person who was currently awake.

She sat down on the edge of the couch next to where Mark was laying on the floor so that she could talk quietly to him and he would be able to hear her hushed tones. He scooted his torso back away from the couch so that he could turn towards her and give her feet some room. She bent down and leaned close to his ear, "my phone was left on all night in the kitchen. Did you leave it on?" His face morphed into any angry mask. "Um, no I am not in the habit of wandering around in the middle of the night wasting what little electricity we have." He answered sarcastically. She was taken aback by his response and physically moved away from him. "I just needed to ask," was her response. He changed his demeanor immediately, "I'm sorry Regan, I didn't sleep very well, bad dreams and this floor is so uncomfortable." He offered as an apology. They were all reaching the end of their proverbial rope. This meant they were running low on patience, but had an abundance of sarcasm to share with each other.

She relaxed a little, "I know, we weren't meant to sleep on floors with children who are restless sleepers." She motioned to the kids still asleep. "I just don't know who would have left it on." She imagined Ainslie playing a game on it as an escape from the boredom or Josh trying to search the internet for some kind of video game information. While at the same time they weren't the kind of kids who would do something like that without asking. They had always asked for everything to the point that it was ridiculous. Ainslie had asked her mother once if she could jump in a snow bank when they were out walking the dogs. She had been bundled up in her snowsuit so that she could play in the snow; it was the whole purpose of the walk. Regan had been dumbfounded at her daughter's request. And Josh had once asked if he could have some peanuts that were put out for snacks at his Aunt's house during a visit. Maybe that was reasonable if he was thinking he'd spoil his dinner. The thought of them going behind her back during a time like this and wasting a valuable resource just seemed so out of character that Regan was having trouble rationalizing it.

"Sam heard from my folks," she told her husband. "Oh yeah? How?" he asked. "Get this, they have power. Can you believe that?" Regan responded. "My dad broke his foot though; he was bringing in some firewood and dropped it." Mark nodded his head, he didn't seem happy they were okay either. "I was a little resentful to hear they had their power back," she said. "Shouldn't the suburbs be the first back online?" She asked him not really expecting him to know. He just shrugged and said, "Who knows how these things work."

Regan gazed out the front window and realized that the snow must have started again at some point during the night as the house that had burned to the ground was now a white mound with no evidence of what had taken place showing. She felt a little better knowing that the skeletal remains of the house couldn't be seen.

As if on cue, large fluffy flakes started to fall from the sky. The way they fell was beautiful and hypnotic. It was almost as if they were dancing to the ground. Mark followed Regan's gaze to the window and muttered, "Jesus," at the sight of the snow falling. He turned away from the window lying on his back and closed his eyes draping his arm over them.

The kids slept on into the morning and Regan left them.

They would get up when they were hungry or needed to pee. Regan made Mark and herself some peanut butter on bread and considered never buying peanut butter again. It felt like they were living off of the stuff. Mark joined her in the kitchen and sat at the table with his bread in front of him looking at it sulkily.

"Fucking peanut butter," he said to the room. Folding the slice of bread in half, he ate only two bites. He knew that he needed the energy and that he should eat, but what he wouldn't give for a nice prime rib cooked medium with a baked potato and a side of broccoli followed by a beer. The thought of that made his mouth water, but instead he used the extra saliva to break down the bread his mouth, thick with peanut butter. "Thanks," he said to his wife sitting across from him. He stood up and put his plate on the counter; no point in wasting it, he hadn't spilled anything on it. He saw Regan's phone lying on the counter and picked it up turning it over in his hands. "Maybe it turned itself on," he suggested sliding it back across the counter to where it had been resting. "I don't know," she replied clearly not wanting to discuss it. "Did you finish the book last night?" he inquired. Regan looked up at him and had to think for a minute what he was talking about, "Oh the Harry Potter one? Yes, we are on to the next one now." Mark nodded his head, "make sure one of the kids gets the next one before dark tonight." She said she would and he went back into the living room.

Regan realized at that moment that she was the one who left the phone on. Josh had called her name last night just before bed when she was in the kitchen throwing away the dinner garbage. She remembered holding the phone and putting it down, but she couldn't remember turning it off. She must have left it on. She felt like such a dumbass for thinking it was somebody else.

She could hear the kids talking to Mark in the living room and quickly spread some peanut butter on some more bread, then carried it into the living room.

Ainslie and Josh both ate quickly and went to their bedrooms to forage for some new entertainment. It seemed that the games and toys that they'd been using for the past few days had lost their luster as well as the living room environment. Josh found Hungry Hungry Hippos and ran to his sister's room to play it. The next half hour was filled with the aggressive clacking of plastic hippo heads slamming the platform they rested on and shouting, with cheers of triumph sprinkled in here and there.

Regan told Mark that she had solved the mystery of the phone that was left on and admitted that it was her. He was good about it and didn't get too high and mighty, just took the battery out of the back of the device and told her that she would need to ask permission to use the phone until she proved that she could be more responsible, all the while grinning at her. She just smirked at him then tried to grab the battery back but he held it high above his head and she had no chance of reaching it with him standing six foot one and she at five foot four there was no chance.

At around eleven, Mark wandered down to the washroom and decided to check on the kids. He peeked through the crack of the door and saw Ainslie dressed up in her best princess dress complete with white evening gloves and little heels, serving imaginary tea from her teapot to her brother who was also dressed up. It was all Mark could do not to laugh out loud at his son. He didn't want to disturb the setting, but his son looked quite ridiculous. He had on a tiara, some kind of pink frilly gown that was open at the back because it was too small for him, black evening gloves and a little sequined hand bag around his wrist sitting at Ainslie's drawing table telling her how delighted he was to be joining her for tea. Mark walked away before either of them would notice that he was there. He couldn't help but be proud of his son. Mark hadn't had sisters, just a brother and all he could remember about his older brother was how annoyed he would get that Mark would always want to follow him around. Josh was different when it came to Ainslie. He had a real soft spot for his little sister. He knew how to push her buttons at times, but then there were the moments like these when he was so good to her. It had to be how close they were in age. Mark was four years younger than his brother, Regan was two years younger than her sister and Josh was just eighteen months older than Ainslie. "I guess that's the sweet spot," he thought to himself.

Mark went to the washroom, did his thing, and then went back to the living room to share what he had seen with his wife with a big, goofy smile spread across his face.

Regan was playing with the dogs, throwing tennis balls for Caesar to catch and the "Daily growl" for Scamp to fetch. The poor animals were getting no exercise being cooped up in the house all day. She decided to go to the stairs and drop Scamp's squeaky toy down them for him to chase after, sure that the act would wear the little dog out. He bolted after the toy, tearing down the stairs as fast as his little legs would take him. When he reached the bottom, Regan heard him slide then a thud, followed by a thud. She stood silently for a moment, unsure if he was okay or not. Then came the squeak of the toy and Scamp came bounding up the stairs, the plastic newspaper poking out of his mouth. Regan decided not to do that again.

Mark came down the hall grinning at her as though he had a secret. "What?" she asked when he was close enough.

"Your son is dressed up and having tea with his sister." Regan smiled and said, "That's so nice." Mark held up his hand to stop her, "no, you don't understand, he is all decked out in a tiara and dress." Regan made a face at him and said, "Really?" He waved at her to follow him and they both crept up to the door and Regan peeked in. She covered her mouth and hurried back to the living room. "That is so sweet," she said in a high whiney voice. "Isn't it?" Mark responded. They both stood together marveling at their children and left them to have fun.

Nobody was very hungry for lunch, having slept in and eaten breakfast late, so Regan used the remaining carrots, cucumber and ranch dip for them to eat as a snack.

The kids had brought some board games from their rooms and were intent on playing all of them before the end of day. Mark and Regan decided to make a point of joining in and making it a family game day. They tried to figure out Chinese checkers, but no one knew how to play so it turned into a game of marbles on the floor. Then came operation, followed by an explanation to Ainslie why the game had electricity but they didn't, leaving the little girl confused but happy that her favorite game was working. By that time Regan and Mark took a step back and let the kids have fun on their own as the games that remained were a little too easy and Mark took a firm stance against letting anybody win.

Regan had really enjoyed her day so far, a stark contrast to yesterday and the events that had unfolded. She didn't let her mind dwell too long on it; she just couldn't do it just yet. Once everything was back to normal, she would allow herself to go to pieces, but not until then.

Mark watched Regan. She seemed genuinely happy, but

he was still worried about her. Yesterday had been such a dark day and he had caught her a few times looking out the window at the snow covered spot where the twins' house had burned down. He was enjoying today as well. It was as if everyone was in the same frame of mind and making the most of the time they had together. He was hoping that they wouldn't have to face any more events like yesterday. Even the living room felt warmer, but that could have just been in his mind. He thought of Regan's parents and realized that the news of them had given the family hope. They were holding on to the fact that power was being restored around them and knew that it was just a matter of time before their turn would come.

# 9 DAY FOUR - AFTERNOON

*Having gas in your car means that you can get to a local school or YMCA , really any location that is serving as shelter from your power outage, or even a hospital if needed. It really is a good rule of thumb to make sure that your tank is always at least half full. It offers peace of mind, and in the winter, condensation can build up in your gas tank causing the fuel lines to freeze. Who knew being prepared can help your everyday life.-Survival Tips for the Urban Idiot*

A loud CRRAACKK broke their silence followed by the sound of glass breaking. The dogs took off barking down the hall to investigate the noise followed by Regan and Mark. The sound had come from their master bedroom.

Upon entering the room the scene was difficult to comprehend. There were tree limbs, snow, and glass everywhere. The bed had been shoved about a foot from where it usually stood and it wasn't lined up with the wall as it had been the last time they were in there. The window looked like the tree had exploded through it, the shattered wooden frame facing inward like broken jagged teeth. Mark went to have a closer look, being careful where he walked so that he didn't end up cutting his foot open.

He put his hand against the wall, leaning over a large part of tree and sighed heavily, his track pants blowing in the wind now coming through the gap. The birch on the front lawn had finally given in to the weight of the ice and snow on it. The fact that it had doubled over gave it the momentum to uproot itself and the weight to crash through the master bedroom making it look like a bomb had gone off. Mark gave another huge sigh. They thought they had escaped any kind of tree catastrophe when the birch had folded over on itself, but obviously they were wrong.

The room temperature had already started to drop. Mark, pushing past Regan, shooed the dogs out of the room and shut the door. "We have to try and keep the cold out," he explained to his wife who was standing on the side of the bed closest to the door and furthest from the tree.

"What are we going to do about this?" she asked him, the fear evident on her face. He just shrugged and said, "We need to get the tree out and try to seal up the opening." Regan couldn't even think. "I have my chainsaw downstairs; maybe I can cut it up enough and then push it outside. Do we have any cardboard?" he asked his wife, Regan didn't respond, entranced by the scene, "Regan, babe. Cardboard, do we have any?" She snapped out of her fog, "Um, I'm not sure," she hesitated then said, "Oh, wait the TV box is still downstairs in the back basement but I'm not sure if it will be big enough." He looked at the scene," it will have to do; we can maybe cut it open so that it's flat." Regan nodded in agreement and Mark said, "okay, let's go get the chainsaw, and the box. We have to make sure to keep this door closed. The last thing we need is someone getting hurt on some of this glass." What he didn't say was, if that should happen, we are fucked. There's no way of getting off the street and no way for anyone to come and help us.

Regan snapped her fingers remembering, "We have those plastic painters' drop cloths. We can use those to seal it up too." "Great idea," he said, "let's go."

They needed to work fast. The huge tree would act as an ice box bringing the temperature down fast in the room and although the wind didn't seem as bad today it was still blowing. Every degree it dropped was a big loss.

The kids were in the hall with the two dogs. "What was that noise?" Josh asked seeing his parents emerge from the room, bristling at the cold coming from the open door. "The window broke," his father replied, "we need you guys to stay out of this room while me and your mom clean it up, okay?" Josh nodded; Ainslie didn't say anything, she just stood beside Caesar with her little hand on his back. "And keep the dogs out as well, okay bud?" Mark nodded to his son to ensure he understood the importance of what he was saying, "Okay dad, you got it," he responded. "Come on Ains, let's go play trouble." The little girl let her brother lead her away.

In that moment, Regan was so proud of her boy. He was being so grown up in this situation, but she was worried about Ainslie. The little girl was not only seeking comfort from the huge dog, she also had her thumb in her mouth, a habit that her mother hadn't seen her do since she was three years old. Occasionally Regan found her in the morning with the digit stuck in her mouth, but it was usually after a rough night. The situation was clearly getting to Ainslie. Regan made a mental note to spend some time with her daughter after the window clean-up was complete.

Following Mark, Regan headed downstairs while the children went back to the safety of the living room with their canine companions. The adults stopped in the kitchen to grab a flashlight each. The chainsaw was in the basement as well as the box and the plastic drop cloths, but if the chainsaw didn't have gas, that would mean having to go out to the garage. They didn't have a door from the house directly into the garage, so someone (probably Mark) would have to go outside. She hoped to god there was gas in the chainsaw.

The back basement was cold and the bare concrete floor had actual patches of ice forming over it, so they walked slowly. Even with each of them in treaded slippers there was no point in risking an injury. Her mind kept going back to the possibility that an ambulance may not be able to get to them.

It didn't take long to find the items needed as well as a brand new role of duct tape. They took their treasures upstairs to the master bedroom door, grabbing Mark's parka, ski mask, boots and heavy duty gloves along the way. The basement was getting too cold to be in for a long period of time. They made their way down the hallway to the door that led into what used to be their cozy little bedroom.

Mark knew that the first thing needed would be cutting up the tree enough to get it out of the house. He shook the chainsaw to see if he could hear the gasoline sloshing around inside. They both looked at each other as they heard the sound of liquid. It was all Mark could do not to jump up and down with excitement; he would take the small victories as they came. He put on his jacket, gloves, mask and boots and opened the door to the room, disappearing inside. Regan stayed put knowing that he would call her if he needed her, no sense in both of them freezing.

She could hear the pull of the rip cord on the chainsaw, nothing happened. He pulled it again, nothing again. She crossed her fingers and silently wished for the machine to come to life. Still nothing happened. Slumping her shoulders, she went to get her Parka, gloves and boots. The next step would be going to the garage when rrrrrr, the chainsaw started up. "phew," she said to herself, but just in case, grabbed her outer clothes from the front door and headed back to the room sitting down outside of the bedroom door to wait for his instruction.

For what seemed like hours, Mark hacked at the tree, its frozen limbs not wanting to give in as the rotating chain ripped into the soft white bark. His hands screaming in protest at the tight grip they held on the tool, vibrations running up his arms. Taking a step back, he noted that he had only severed a few branches from the trunk, there was a lot more to get through.

He stopped for a moment and wiped the back of his gloved hand across his sweaty forehead to stop the drips from going into his eyes. Lifting the chainsaw over his head, he brought it down onto a thick limb that would clear a small hole to the outside. "Progress, yes'" he thought to himself. He used his weight to push the little machine down and through the wood. It went on like that for a while using brute force to chop up the tree.

Before long, he had cut off all of the branches and limbs that had invaded his bedroom. The only intact part of the tree was the trunk that was angled into the window. He was concerned that the chainsaw was not powerful enough to handle the thicker mass of the trunk, but there was nothing else he could do.

"Rrrrrr," the chainsaw chugged and then stopped dead. "Oh shit," he said, trying to pull the tool from the trunk. It was stuck in the tree. He tried sawing it back and forth and then with a snap the chain broke. "JESUS!" Mark roared. He was so close. He started kicking and thrashing around snapping and crushing the remnants of the tree lying on the bedroom's carpet.

"Mark," Regan called, hearing the commotion. She entered the room to see what had happened. Her husband stared at her, and she closed the door staying in the room. Breathing heavily he lifted his arms up, "I give up!" he declared, "I was so fucking close and the god damn thing ran out of gas I think. Then to add insult to injury the chain broke." She could see the chainsaw sticking out of the tree trunk with the chain dangling from it.

"Mark," she said a little quieter. "I know, I know," he said, " I need to calm down, get my head straight blah, blah fucking blah," he replied sarcastically and swatted at a branch that hadn't been broken in his rant. "Mark," she tried a little more stern. He stopped everything and turned to look at her. She had gone pale. "Your leg," she said pointing to his left leg. There was a huge piece of glass sticking out of it, his pant leg already soaking red with blood. "Oh Jesus," he said breathlessly and instinctively went to pull it out. "No," Regan called to him, but it was too late. He had yanked the jagged piece out of his flesh and blood started to flow freely. He looked pleadingly at his wife and partly fell, partly sat on their bed. At first, anger flashed through her. He was sitting on their expensive comforter. Then the reality of the situation hit her and she pulled a sheet from the bed and quickly tied it tightly around the wound, trying to put pressure on it to stem the flow of blood. "It's okay," she tried to reassure him, seeing as he looked terrified and could probably use the comfort. "I'm going to get the first aid kit," he reached for her, but she disappeared down the hall. Time was of the essence in a situation like this.

Josh saw her with bloody hands and his eyes went the size of saucers, while Ainslie thankfully had her back to her mother and was preoccupied by something. Regan put her finger to her lips and her son nodded understanding what she wanted him to do. He chatted animatedly to his little sister as if everything were okay, Regan needed him to distract the little girl otherwise the scene could become a whole lot more dramatic.

Regan snatched the first aid kit from the kitchen counter, and running down the hall, went to her husband's aid. He was lying on the bed staring at the ceiling, avoiding the sight of his leg. In her absence, he had pulled off his ski mask and gloves; they were lying beside him on the bed. He had always been a bit squeamish; lucky for him, Regan was not.

"Okay," she said, taking the scissors out of the red box, she cut his pant leg up to his thigh. The blood looked like it had slowed, "good," she thought, "he must not have hit an artery then." She kept those thoughts to herself though. Good news or not, any update would probably upset him, unless it were her saying that he was all fixed up now. Leaving the room again, she headed for the bathroom to wash her hands and soak some face cloths to clean the wound.

Once the water had done its job, she opened a bottle and poured some alcohol onto a gauze bandage and laid it on the open wound. It seemed deep and she thought he might need stitches. "I've just cleaned it up and put a bandage on. The bleeding should stop soon," she said, practicing her first aid speak. "Okay," he mumbled. She knew he would be beating himself up mentally, telling himself things like, "how could you be so stupid?" and "what were you thinking?" Regan wished he could think more like her and accept the fact that accidents happen and this could have happened to anyone. Although, in the back of her mind she also knew that he lost control of his anger, and because of that, he is hurt and it could have been even worse. It was so important for them to keep their emotions in check right now.

Once she was done, Regan sat back to admire her work. "Does it hurt?" she asked. "Nah, it's okay," he responded. "Well let me know if it starts to hurt, there is a bottle of pain relievers in here," she said holding up the little white bottle of Advil, the pills inside creating that distinct clicking sound.

She helped him to his feet and let him lean on her while she walked him out to the couch. "Elevate that leg and try not to move around," she was telling him as she helped him ease himself onto the sofa and slipped off his jacket and boots. The kids were on him as soon as he appeared. "Are you okay daddy?" Ainslie asked. "Yes sweetheart, I'll be fine. Just a little boo boo." Josh came for a closer look, "did the chainsaw do that to you?" Mark smiled at his son. The boy had feared the tool since he was little, Mark knew that fear would keep him vigilant in his later life. "No bud, it was a piece of glass from the window. I didn't even notice it."

Regan left her husband in the children's hands as another distraction to get them through the day. She went back into the bedroom, the tree mockingly stuck through the window. The first thing she did was put on Mark's big gloves and pick up the big pieces of glass, putting them in the cardboard TV box. "Better in the box, they won't tear through it like they would a garbage bag," she thought to herself. Then she gathered all of the tree debris and bundled them together using the duct tape. She put the bundles in the corner of her room out of the way. The tree trunk loomed over her; she was not sure what to do about that. Leaning her shoulder against it she tried to push with all of her might, but the tree wouldn't budge. She ended up having to leave it where it was. Kicking the jagged window frame outside, she was able to make a clear space where she hung the plastic sheet. She taped it along the top of the wall while she stood on one of the side tables to reach. Then she sealed up the other edges of the sheet with the tape, creating a make-shift wall. The tree protruded into the plastic about a foot so the plastic was not completely flat, but at least the wind couldn't get in. She did the same with three more drop sheets, making a thicker wall in the hopes of better insulating the room. She was happy with the progress and left the room, taking all of her supplies, including the first aid kit, with her. She left the large box in the room. No point in introducing dangers to the youngsters in the house, and she wasn't going to risk carrying it out to the garage right now.

They had canned spaghetti for dinner with the last of the bread. Regan used the barbeque to heat the pasta, can and all, remembering to remove the paper label so as not to start a fire. Then, using the tongs, she removed the can once the sauce started to boil a little. The thought of fire brought the twins back to mind, but she shook it off. Her family needed her now more than ever. She couldn't go down that depressing road today. She laid the bread on the grill. It didn't need to be toasted, but she liked the idea that if there was any mold or bacteria starting to form, toasting the slices may kill it off. The rest of the evening was spent with the kids doting on their father, telling jokes and stories, followed by another couple of chapters from their book. Josh loved to read just like his mother, and Ainslie seemed to be heading down the same path. Regan smiled as she thought of the time when they were younger and she would climb into their beds and read a story every night, no matter what was happening. All of those tired nights had paid off.

The night passed uneventfully to Regan's relief. She was the last to fall asleep as usual, but she slept deeply this time along with her family in the cold quiet house.

# 10 DAY FIVE - MORNING

*Canned goods are your friend. When the produce in your fridge has either been consumed or has rotted and turned grey giving off a putrid stench that makes your compost bin smell like daisies, it is time to turn to your cupboards and all those canned goods you were going to give to the food bank on your kids next food drive. You know the tuna that you bought with the hopes of getting your omega threes or that tin of corn you purchased only to discover a week after you bought it that it is creamed corn, yuck! – Survival Tips for the Urban Idiot*

The wind had picked up again, whipping the snow violently against the window and blowing it in various directions throughout the street. They had all slept through the night. Regan and the kids on the floor while Mark was on the couch; they figured it would be better for his leg to be away from the kids. She didn't want him to tear his wound open because of the kids' thrashing around at night.

Although Regan had slept the entire night, she still felt tired. The last four nights might be catching up with her, or maybe she didn't have a restful sleep. It was as if she had blinked and the night was over. At least she had not been plagued by nightmares or horrible images. That reassurance didn't seem to help much. She felt no urgency to get up or try to reach her boss, resigned to the fact that she would receive no answer if she tried. Even if she did manage to get through, what was she going to say? It would be impossible to get out of her driveway, let alone the street. And there was no way she was going to let her kids go to school in this.

Regan peered out the window. It was difficult just to see through to the front yard, but across the street was even worse. All she could see was fuzzy whiteness. She tried all the same, squinting her eyes, straining to make out any landmark. At one point, she thought she saw someone out there walking up the street, but upon second glance there was no one. The snow was playing tricks on her. She chalked it up to the snow casting shadows. "Who would be out in this?" She questioned herself. In the end, she let it go and turned away.

The sun was poking through the clouds; at least that was some progress. She put her slippers on and grabbed her hoodie that was lying on the couch. She stretched her sore body. The kinks were there every morning, but they seemed to be getting better or maybe she was just getting used to them being there. She then checked on Mark's leg. Lifting the blankets that covered him gently so as not to disturb him. She could see where the blood had seeped through his pajama leg. "I'll have to change that dressing and see what's going on," she said to herself, then headed down the hall to the bathroom.

The light switch loomed ahead of her, it had become her nemesis. Every day she would fill with hope only to be deflated by the little toggle, but she had to check. Right now, it was her marker; it determined how her day was going to go. Putting her hand on the switch she said a little prayer, "please god, let the power come back on today. I can't take much more of this uncertainty. Please, please let this storm be over so we can get Mark to a hospital. I really don't know what I'm doing here." With that she flicked the switch. Nothing happened. Her hand dropping to her side she punched her thigh from sheer frustration.

Regan thought about trying to get an update from the radio in the kitchen, but they had only received static for the past two days. The signal was either lost or the station had run out of power and was no longer broadcasting. The cheap little radio couldn't pick up stations that were further away. She wished that she had helped the kids with that Christmas present, giving them a little more money toward it or helped with the research of what to buy. It might have made a difference in this situation, but how was she to know at the time. An old saying came back to her: if ifs and buts were candy and nuts, we'd all have a merry Christmas. She shook her head, "where had that come from?" she wondered to herself.

In the bathroom, the toilet bowl had started to turn a scummy yellow. Implementing the "if its yellow, let it mellow, if its brown flush it down," rule was taking a toll on the porcelain. They had only used a quarter of the tub water for flushing which was pretty good. The bottled water on the other hand was starting to run low. Regan had become somewhat of a water Nazi, ensuring that not even a drop was wasted. Before the blackout, her kids would easily waste half a bottle pouring it down the sink as it was warm or they didn't want it anymore. She was pretty sure that they could drink the bathtub water once the bottles were gone, but she needed to check with Mark on that. "We don't have a water softener and we are on a city system so it should be all right", she rationalized. The dogs seem to be okay munching on the snow. Regan had started taking the chunks that Scamp brought in and divvying them up into the dog's water bowls so she didn't have to use her precious bottled water.

After she relieved herself, Regan stood looking in the large mirror over the sink. Her shoulder length blond hair looked greasy and unkempt pulled back in a mini ponytail. Her clothes looked oversized on her giving the impression that she had either shrunk or had lost a large amount of weight quickly and her eyes were hollow and blackened underneath. Not a very good look. She was so tired and as she stared into the mirror, tears welled up in her green eyes. The darkened bathroom allowed her eyes to play tricks on her. The face in the mirror shifted and morphed into different people, a monster, an old man, a weathered lady, was this really only the fifth day? It was pretty sad how dependent they had become on electricity. She hoped that after this experience she would remain vigilant and implement some activities that would allow her and her family to be a little more independent of "the grid." But if she were being honest with herself, life was hard and anything that made it easier to get along was exploited. So that was where they would end up after this storm was over, right back where they started whether she wanted to admit it right now or not.

"I will not break," she told the stranger reflecting back at her softly. "Everything will be okay," her voice held no reassurance, so she tried to smile but her face grimaced into a woman who was about to cry. She put her hands on either side of the sink and let her head fall forward trying to gather herself together. The motion ended up stretching the muscles that held up her head making them scream in relief. Her fingers stretched and gripped the sink while her back cracked up her spine. "Aw," she let out a cry at the shock of her back realigning. Her body felt better.

Turning to the tub, she scooped up some water with the little toy bucket they had been using to transport the flushing water from the tub to the toilet. Setting the bucket on the counter she dipped her hands into the water and splashed it onto her face. It was ice cold and Regan gasped as it made contact with her skin. That seemed to wake her up a little.

She looked in the mirror again, and this time the image looking back at her appeared more like herself. Well, at least she could see more of who she was reflecting back. "One day you might even look back on this time with fond memories," she told herself. Her thoughts floated back to the house that had burned down across the street and the possibility that two woman had died while Regan's family slept comfortably. "Maybe not," she concluded and exited the bathroom.

Mark was telling the kids to leave him alone when Regan entered the room, "what's up?" she asked. He looked up at her pale, tired and sweaty. "Oh shit," she thought to herself, "I hope he doesn't have a fever. That could mean an infection and then I don't know what to do." He was shoving the blankets down with his arms, "why did you put so many blankets on me?" he asked clearly frustrated. She went to his side, and holding the back of his head with her hand, she noted that he did feel warm, but wasn't hot. She breathed a little easier at that. "I didn't want you to get cold without us," was her response as she helped him remove the covers.

"Can I look at the leg?" she asked, pointing at the bandage. "Looks like it has been bleeding again." He lay back as she pulled back the blankets to have a look. Gently, she lifted the leg of his track pants and peeled the bandage back. He winced as she pulled the tape from his skin. The wound opened again as she pulled off the dressing.

He took one look at her face and said, "what is it?" She wore a look of disapproval as she inspected the damage. "It keeps opening. I think you need stitches." He did not like the sound of that without a shot to numb his leg, this would probably hurt quite a bit. "Let me go get the first aid kit," she said to him and left the room.

Ainslie stood staring at his torn flesh. "Oh honey, don't look at that," he said waving her over to him. He positioned her so that her back was facing the wound and she was looking at his face. "Are you going to be okay daddy?" she asked fiddling with her hands; it was as if she couldn't look at him. "Of course I am." He hoped so. "Mommy is just going to do some first aid so that I don't get sick from my cut." He told her.

Regan returned with the first aid kit. "Ainslie honey, why don't you go into the kitchen? Josh found some Cheerios." The little girl started to leave the room, but stopped in the doorway to look back at her parents. Regan didn't notice, but Mark did and he smiled at the little girl who then ran away.

"Okay, there is a needle in here, but no thread. I'm not sure how much this is going to hurt." Mark thought he was going to pass out just thinking about what she wanted to do to him. "I don't think I can handle it Regan," he told her. "Don't be silly, you'll be fine. Would you rather bleed to death?" she asked, not totally sure herself that she could do this. Making a stuffed animal in Home Economics was one thing, but the thought of sewing human flesh sent a shiver down her spine.

Mark saw the crazy glue in the first aid kit. "Wait what is that for?" he asked. His wife hadn't noticed it at first. "Remember that show we watched and they used glue instead of stitches?" He asked her. "Yes," she replied, "but it didn't always work," she commented. "Well, why don't we try it and if it doesn't work, then we'll do the stitching thing," he swallowed deep and hoped she would side with him. She stopped with the needle in her hand and considered his request, "it had worked," she thought to herself. "okay," she replied, "but that means we will need to immobilize your leg so that it has a chance to dry," she said getting up.

"Not a problem," he breathed a sigh of relief.

Regan would need two pieces of wood and some rope or tape to keep his leg straight while she applied the glue and waited for it to dry. She remembered the discarded pieces of tree still in her bedroom that would be perfect. "Okay, I'll be right back," she told her husband and went in search of two relatively long pieces of wood.

She ventured back into their bedroom to salvage some branches. The plastic that was covering the gaping hole that was once their window had held up pretty well. One corner that was exposed to the outside was flapping in the wind, but the other layers had held, and no wind was getting in. The room was still significantly colder than the rest of the house. Her thoughts turned to her jacket at the front door, not doing her any good hanging all the way over there. She pulled the hood of her sweater up and went to work undoing the first bundle of branches that still sat in the corner. Most of the wood was inadequate for the job so she considered getting the axe and splitting some of the thicker trunk pieces. Frustrated, she fastened the duct tape back around the branches, then kneeling on the floor for a minute, tried to come up with an alternative when she noticed that one of the slates from the bed was dislodged. She went over and shoved the mattress aside and discovered some of the slates had broken, she presumed it had happened when the tree came through the window. Taking one slate that was almost broken in half; she examined it and figured it would work.

Taking her find with her, she headed back out to the living room, stopping to ensure that the bedroom door was closed up tight. Standing in the hallway, she could feel a draft coming from under the door. "I could probably take some duct tape and seal it up," Regan thought to herself. She contemplated the task and decided it was something for later, making a mental note to come back and deal with the door after she patched Mark up.

Making quick work of the splint, she used the duct tape to hold the wood slates in place. It wasn't pretty, but it would do the job. The next step was to apply the glue. She gently tried to separate the skin and squeezed the glue onto the left side of the skin, and then pressed the separated flesh together while Mark looked away grimacing. Once finished, she left the wound uncovered in the hopes that it would dry faster. Sure enough, after leaving it for ten minutes, it seemed to have fused the skin closed. Regan gently removed the splint and applied a clean bandage to Mark's leg. Then brought him some of the Cheerios the kids had found. He smirked at her, no doubt feeling like a child being waited on hand and foot; it was just too bad she didn't have any suckers.

The wind stayed wild all morning, blocking much of the street from view. The charred remains of the twins' house now lay covered in snow. You couldn't even tell that a house had once stood there. This came as a relief to Regan because she didn't want the constant reminder that always seemed to lead to her wondering what had happened to the ladies. It was easier to avoid thinking about them with Mark being hurt. She was too busy for thoughts of that caliber. However, the intense feeling of loss was right on the edge of Regan's subconscious, threatening to overwhelm her at any moment.

The kids were getting antsy and begged to play in the basement, to which Regan reluctantly said yes. It was cold down there and they had to wear their outside gear including boots. At that point, they would have agreed to anything. The running around would do them good, wear them out and keep them warm. Caesar went down the stairs with them, but Scamp stayed with Mark. The little dog seemed to think he had to protect him, from what, Regan had no idea. The little dog would march up and down the couch then when he was satisfied that Mark was not in danger, he would circle the same spot at Mark's feet and settle down with his head resting on his paws for a little while until his next patrol.

The kids had been wearing the same clothes now for a few days and Regan was going to make sure both kids had a sponge bath tonight and change into some fresh duds. The thought of the ice cold bath water raised goose bumps on her arms and she thought about filling the sink and warming some of the water on the barbeque. That way it wouldn't be so uncomfortable. She could do it while supper was being made. Efficiency was the name of the game right now, they couldn't afford to waste any resources. Luckily she knew all about that, having developed her multitasking skills since the day they had started their family.

Once the kids went downstairs, Regan enjoyed some time to herself, reading from one of her own books and planning throughout the morning while Mark dosed in and out.

At one point, she remembered the draft coming through the master bedroom door and grabbed the roll of duct tape.

Dropping to her knees on the floor, she put her hand up to the gap between the bottom of the floor and the carpet. There was definitely a gust of cold air coming through. She screeched out a good sized strip of duct tape and tore the piece away from the roll with her teeth. Then, she pressed it against the door and the carpet. At first, she wasn't sure that it would stick to the carpet, but after sticking a few layers down, it held. She quickly reinforced it with a few more strips just to be sure, and then repeated the same procedure for the rest of the edging around the door. Once complete, she held her hand up to all of the places the air was coming through before and felt nothing. Happy with herself, she returned to the living room and her book.

It was almost one o'clock before the children came back upstairs out of breath and sweating, even Caesar was panting heavily.

# 11 DAY FIVE - AFTERNOON

*If you have a first aid kit, good for you! Do you know how to use the stuff inside? Even if you do, why not take a first aid course at your local St. John's Ambulance or Red Cross. Learn how to treat minor injuries and perform CPR if needed. Some employers will even pay for an employee to take the course. The techniques are always changing and a refresher is never a bad idea. – Survival Tips for the Urban Idiot*

By the time the kids returned, the wind had died down considerably and Regan let the dogs out on the deck for a pee. She pointed to the back corner of the wooden structure and the canines obliged and relieved themselves far enough from the barbeque and the main area that she had been using for Regan to feel comfortable. They were quick about it and she tried her best to open and close the sliding door quickly. Although the wind had died down, the temperature was still frigid and without a heat source the house was not staying warm as it had.

She returned to the living room to huddle with the kids when something outside the window caught her eye. There was something black lying in the road. She couldn't make it out and resolved it to be somebody's garbage that had blown into the middle of the street, now being anchored by the heavy pile of snow that had collected on top of it.

Feeling much better after some rest and Regan's treatment, Mark had started to hobble around a bit. The glue seemed to be working to Regan's relief. He went to the kitchen to get himself some water. He seemed restless, walking back and forth in front of the window. "I know you don't want to stiffen up, but make sure you don't overdo it," Regan said to him.

Mark went to the middle window staring at the outdoors, as a trapped animal would eye its freedom. He stood looking out at the street as Regan played Clue for the millionth time with Josh and Ainslie. "Regan, did you see that?" he asked pointing outside. "Yeah," she said, not even bothering to look up, "must be somebody's garbage that blew into the street."

"Um… I don't think so," he replied. Something in his voice made her look up. His eyes were huge and he nodded his head towards the window as if to say take another look.

Annoyed, she uncovered her blanketed legs and went to stand beside him. "What?" She asked somewhat exasperated. He pointed to the bag in the street, but the snow had drifted and there was a very distinct shape revealing itself. This was definitely not a bag of garbage, but the form of a gloved hand. A lime green gloved hand.

"Oh my god," Regan gasped. Her hands instinctively covering her mouth as if to push the words back in. Ainslie turned to look at her mother and asked, "what is it mommy?"

"It's nothing honey just a bag of garbage in the street," she reassured her daughter, but Regan could feel the goose bumps forming on her arm and the blood draining from her face. Could it be Mr. Fulton out there? If it was him there was no way they could help him now, was there? He was totally buried in the snow except for his arm.

"We have to go check," Mark said as if reading her mind. She just nodded in response. Mark was already heading for the front door, Regan followed. He put on his snow pants, big snow mobile boots and parka. Regan tried to stop him, "you're hurt, let me go," she laid her hand on his arm. He just shook his head, "You wouldn't be able to carry him if he needs help," was his response to her. She knew he was right. "Are you sure you can go out there with your leg?" he looked down at his leg while limping around and gathering his things. Then he said, "I'll be fine, just keep an eye on me so you can open the door when I come back." She handed him the gloves that he'd been wearing from the living room, and then went into the little wooden box that they kept all of the heavy duty gloves and hats in, handing him a ski mask to protect his face and goggles so that he would be able to see, and finally, some heavier waterproof gloves. She didn't like this, but she knew him enough to know that there was nothing she could do or say to stop him.

When he was ready, he yanked the door open. It took three tries to get the stubborn, frozen door to budge. Once it did, he trudged off into the snow. Regan quickly slammed the door and hurried back to the living room to watch the events that were about to unfold.

"Where is dad going?" Josh asked from behind her. "Um, he is going to move that garbage bag. Can you take my turn for me? I just want to make sure your dad is okay." Josh gave her a puzzled look, shrugged his shoulders, and muttered an okay. "I want to go outside too." Ainslie declared standing up facing her mother "No honey it is still too dangerous." Regan told her daughter and guided her by the shoulder back to the board game making sure that neither one of them saw the scene outside.

It took Mark ten minutes just to reach what would have been the end of their driveway. He battled through waist high drifts and precarious hidden ice, as well as the occasional dip that once sent him into the snow up to his shoulders. She could see he was out of breath by the puffs that hung in the air from his mouth and he was stopping frequently to catch his breath. She hoped that his leg would hold, but had real doubts. This was far too strenuous, especially for such a fresh wound.

Fifteen minutes later, he had reached the arm sticking out of the snow. He braced himself, getting ready to yank on the arm in the hopes of freeing the old man. When he pulled, the force threw him back and he fell into the snow, disappearing from sight momentarily. He then sat up and was left holding a disembodied arm. Panic took over and he threw the arm aside, horrified at the possibility that he had just ripped another man's arm off. He got his nerve together and upon closer inspection saw that the arm was already frozen where it had been severed. It looked as though it had indeed been torn off the body by something and there were bite marks down the inside of the arm as if an animal had gotten a hold of it.

Mark went back to the snow pile where the arm had been and got down on his knees. Favoring his injured leg as best he could, he started to dig through the snow much like a dog would.

There was nothing there; he would have hit something pretty fast if a body were buried here. He tried another spot a few feet from where he had just been digging. He knew time was not on his side. He had to make sure to conserve enough energy for the journey back to the house, but the thought of possibly leaving an old man out in the snow to die was too much to bear.

When the second spot turned up nothing, he stood up and kicked at a few other places with his good leg, revealing nothing but more snow. He decided to go back to the house. As difficult as it was, his options were to go back, or risk dying out here. So picking up the arm that was still lying in the snow beside him, he headed back towards the house.

Regan couldn't see what he did with the arm, but figured he left it by the garage for when rescue finally came. He wouldn't want the kids seeing it lying out in the middle of the road. It also seemed like the respectful thing to do.

The thought of the old man wandering around outside and ending up god knows where struck her and she felt the familiar sting of tears in her eyes. "He was once someone's Mark," guilt filled her at the thought of their last encounter. "Would it really have been a bad thing to let him stay," she found it hard to remember why she had felt such hatred for him; it all seemed so silly now.

She ran to the door to meet him, swinging the door open for him in the process. Mark entered the house with a swirl of snow whipping in behind him. She threw herself into her husband's arms, slamming the door closed on her way past. "Are you okay?" she asked desperately. He hugged her back and started to shake. It was that indistinguishable tremor that humans get when emotions take over. She held him knowing that he was crying for both Mr. Fulton's misfortune and the guilt of their last encounter. He muttered some incomprehensible words and she just clung to him.

They stood like that for a few minutes, then Mark let go to wipe his nose with the back of his right gloved hand. He took a deep breath and said, "It was his arm Regan," he told her in a loud whisper, "It was his fucking arm, but where is the rest of him?" He asked bewildered. Regan just shrugged, she didn't know what to say. He needed to get out of those wet clothes and make sure that his leg was okay. That's all she was focusing on at that moment. Unfortunately, something bad had happened to their neighbor, but that didn't mean Mark should suffer any more than he already was. She helped him take off his outer wear and eased him down to sit on the stairs so that she could remove his boots.

She guided him into the kitchen, shutting the bi-fold door so that the kids wouldn't disturb them. They both sat at the table facing each other. "What do you think happened?" she asked knowing he would have seen a lot more then she had. "I don't know," he said, "But the arm had been there a while. It was all frozen and there were bite marks down it. I think something might have tried to eat the arm." Regan felt sick at the thought. "What animal around here would want to eat an arm?" she wondered to herself. He put his head in his hands trying to forget what he had just seen.

"How does your leg feel?" she asked, kneeling on the floor and getting ready to have a look. "Fine," he said pulling away. "Can you just please give me a minute?" he snapped. She backed away standing in the middle of the small room unsure what to do next.

Regan couldn't help but feel hurt. After all, her concern was for his well-being. However, she did understand that what he'd seen had upset him, maybe even traumatized him, so she gave him some time to recover. They both just stayed quiet and still for a little while.

Then Mark presented his leg to her for inspection. That was in some way an apology for being short with her. He had to pull down the track pants he had been wearing and she could see blood soaking through the bandage before even removing it. "Dammit," she muttered to herself. Mark just hung his head in surrender. A part of him knew it was going to be bad news, his posture mirroring his feelings of defeat.

"We could try gluing it again, but this time you can't be active," she told him. The thought of sewing up his leg now terrified her. She had convinced herself that punching more holes into his flesh was just going to create a gateway for infection. In truth, she didn't want to do it. The thought of feeding a needle and thread through his skin made her feel queasy and shook her confidence.

Mark had rested his head on the table, his face turned to look at her. "Whatever you think we should do," he resolved his fate to her. "Let's get you back on the couch and re-do that leg then." She said trying to sound optimistic, "I really think it will be okay if you just stay on the couch."

He stood up with his arm out for her to go under it, becoming his crutch. Then they hobbled out to the living room.

"Did you get it dad?" Josh asked. Mark looked at his son confused, then realization of what he  was talking about dawned. . The 'garbage bag' was what Josh was talking about. Mark tried to mask his gloominess with fatigue and said, "yeah buddy, I got it," and with that he lay on the couch while Regan went to work patching him up.

"Colonel Mustard, with the knife, in the conservatory," Ainslie was announcing to the room. She peeked into the little manila envelope that had occupied the space in the middle of the game board and her shoulders dropped. "Aww," she whined. "I got it wrong." Josh stood up, "well that's game over. Let's do something else," he suggested.

"You guys can help me," Regan suggested. She had just finished placing a clean gauze pad over Mark's wound and was about to tape it into place. "I need to get ready for dinner and I want you guys to have a wash and change into some clean clothes." Ainslie made a face.

"What do you want us to do?" Josh asked excited to help. "Well, can you get a bowl or a pot from the kitchen and fill it with some of the bath water? I'll heat up some water for you guys while dinner is warming up."

Josh disappeared to complete his task. "What about me?" asked Ainslie. "You, my dear, can pick something for dinner. What do you feel like?" Ainslie put her finger to the side of her mouth as if she were thinking about the question. "Can we have some chunky soup?" she asked. "I think that is an excellent choice," her mother replied. "Can you please go get me the can?" Ainslie ran off to complete her task. Regan put the first aid gear back into the box and left it beside the couch, hoping she wouldn't need it again, but keeping it close just in case. She got her outer gear on and went outside to start the barbeque.

Josh got the water and Ainslie got the soup. Once warmed up, Regan carried the hot water to the bathroom and filled the sink for Josh mixing it with some cold bath water to reach the perfect temperature. Then left him to it reminding him twice that he needed to wash EVERYTHING!

A little while later he appeared looking a little cleaner then he had and in some fresh warm clothes which consisted of a t-shirt, sweater, long john's, sweat pants and two pairs of socks.

Then Regan did the same for Ainslie this time re-using the water in the sink she warmed some up and carried the hot water for her mixing it in the sink. Ainslie assured her mother that she could do it herself and once again Regan left the bathroom. The soup would be ready by now.

When Ainslie appeared, she was bundled up in a similar fashion as her brother with the added bonus of her bathrobe being draped over her other clothes. They all sat in the living room eating their soup. Regan had put the stones on the barbeque before turning it off which had become the routine at night. She asked the kids to help her bring them into the living room when they were done. They were very careful not to burn themselves, wrapping the stones in the same linens as the night before. Then they all settled in for the evening's events. Lighting the candles, some conversation, a few laughs, followed by reading a few chapters of the book they were on now. Regan enjoyed this part of the day the most, but dreaded what followed.

She made a mental note that when the hydro came back on they should try to implement this practice at least once a month. It made her feel really connected to her family and they all seemed to enjoy it.

That night, Regan gave Mark an Advil. It was more to help him sleep than to take his pain away. As usual though, the kids passed out while she was reading. She knew Mark was probably going to have trouble sleeping because of his leg and his worries for Mr. Fulton. In the end, it was her who couldn't sleep. She kept on having visions of a one-armed, frozen Mr. Fulton walking up and down the street. "What happened to him?" she wondered, "where was the rest of him?" Her imagination ran wild, "maybe there was a killer on the street." Her thoughts turned to the gaping hole in what used to be her master bedroom and she felt vulnerable, pulling the blanket up to her face for protection.

She knew that Mark had moved the shotgun and shells to the kitchen cupboard that locked, but she was wishing that it was a little closer right now. "Stop it," she scolded herself. "There is nothing to be afraid of except the possibility of this going on much longer." She lay in the dark staring at the ceiling and listening to the different sounds of the night. Scamp had been outside a little earlier and she could hear him slurping on a chunk of snow he had dragged back into the house while Caesar lay close by snoring softly and whimpering every once in a while. She wondered if the large dog was having bad dreams as a result of the past few days. Whenever he would shiver or cry she would place a comforting hand on him and lightly pet the dog until he would go silent.

Regan drifted off to fitful sleep and dreamed of frozen dead men, and burned old ladies even at one point Scamp was in her dream noisily licking what she thought was snow, but ended up being a disembodied arm with a lime green glove covering the end of the appendage.

# 12 DAY SIX - MORNING

*Try to charge your cell phone nightly as a habit, that way if you have juice and a signal, the cell phone can be used for emergencies. Advise your family members to do the same. If you have any teenagers in the house when the power goes out just take the phones away from them, this will save arguments later when they are sending selfies to their friends. It's just easier that way. – Survival Tips for the Urban Idiot*

Always the first one up, Regan crawled out of the make-shift camp. She saw Ainslie was awake, but she was just lying still looking up at her mother.

Regan headed for the bathroom, stopping at the light switch as she had every day for the last six, not really expecting anything, but hoping beyond hope that the bulb would illuminate and they could get back to normal.

She flipped the switch, nothing. Her shoulders sagged and she flipped it down again. Just for confirmation, she looked at the stove clock to ensure that it was still dark. It was.

From behind her, Ainslie started to cry, "you lied to me daddy," she spluttered at her father. "You said the 'lectrictiy would be back on two days ago." Using her sleeve, she wiped her snotty nose. "I'm cold and hungry daddy, make them put it on. I want to watch TV." She wailed. All Mark could do was comfort his daughter. He pulled her into his lap and wrapped his arms around her, making her look so small. "I know honey," he murmured to her, "we all want the power to come back on."

Regan looked at her husband and he stared back lifting his eyebrows as if to say, okay we have another day ahead of us so let's get through it. Regan turned back towards the washroom.

Josh continued to sleep while Scamp and Caesar disappeared out for their morning pee.

Upon returning from the bathroom, Regan went into the kitchen to see what they could have for breakfast. She opened the fridge door and was met by a foul smelling odor. Some of the produce was starting to turn she presumed. She would have to go through the fridge and throw out what was going off, and then put the garbage outside.

She decided the best thing to do was open the fridge door and grab as much stuff as she could then shut the door to try and keep the cold in. As cold as the house was the fridge had started warming up. She managed to quickly clear the shelves leaving the condiments in the door. All of the items on the counter looked bad.

Retrieving a black garbage bag from under the counter brought back the memory of the disembodied arm that was lying outside of her garage door. Her thoughts drifted once again to the possibilities of what happened to Mr. Fulton. There had been no other signs of him. Had something eaten him? Was he buried in a snow bank somewhere to be revealed later? It didn't matter how many options her imagination could come up with, she wouldn't know until she knew.

Mark limped into the kitchen, "yikes." He said looking at all of the food on the counter. "It stinks in here." He picked up some brown, mushy, leafy thing and said, "why didn't we put this stuff in the snow?" Regan looked at him with a mix of surprise and annoyance on her face. "Nobody suggested that," she said grabbing the kale or what she thought was kale out of his hand and shoving it into the garbage bag she held.

She was in no mood for what today had in store. The radio wasn't working, so they couldn't get updates. Her cell phone had finally died due to a lack of power and the bread was all gone. The thought of eating another can of gross processed food was more then she could bear.

The fear of not knowing how long this was going to go on for was the worst part of it. The radio had been their only link to the world beyond their four walls, and now it felt as though they were the last people left alive. Day after day the weather pelted their little house and would not allow anyone in the neighborhood to venture outside. Regan was starting to believe that her community was now gone.

Mark could sense Regan's anger and sat quietly watching her as she threw an assortment of unidentifiable foods into the black garbage bag at her feet. They were all getting fed up. The stress of not knowing the outcome of their situation was weighing heavier with each passing day. The kids were bored and so were Regan and Mark.

She finished dealing with the remnants of food that she had taken out of the fridge and threw everything in the bag, tying it up. Sanitizing her hands, Regan set about looking for a suitable breakfast.

Since there was no bread, the eggs were gone and the remaining fruits and vegetables were inedible, she had to really think outside the box. Opening the cupboard doors, she shoved the remaining canned meals aside. There was nothing on the first shelf so she grabbed a kitchen chair and had a look at the second shelf; it looked pretty bare. On the top shelf stood a lone bag of oatmeal, shoved to the very back. She grabbed the bag. It was still sealed, nobody had ever opened it. "Score!" she thought to herself. There was still a need to venture out into the cold for the water to be boiled, but at least she found something appropriate for them to eat and it would fill them up.

Mark looked outside and the same grey sky hung over them, casting a miserable shadow on their lives and the uncertainty of the future. One saving grace was that it looked like the snow that had been falling quietly that morning had stopped for now.

He felt guilty for being hurt and not able to help Regan as he would have liked to but it wasn't as though he had stuck that piece of glass into his leg on purpose, shit happens. Mark wondered to himself if that was why she seemed so angry this morning and decided that was probably only a drop in the bucket at this point.

Regan got a large pot out of one of the lower cupboards and went to fill it with water for the oatmeal. She was so annoyed with Mark right now. He was just sitting in the kitchen watching her run around like an idiot. Didn't he know how much that bugged her; it was like he was making sure she was doing something. "Just go back out to the living room and leave me alone," she wanted to scream at him, but kept the thought to herself. Instead, she put on all of her gear and went out to the deck to spark up the barbecue.

Once on the deck, she breathed the cool air in. It made her cough a little, but it was nice to be outside. Even though it was cold, she messed around with the barbeque, staying out a bit longer then was necessary. She was afraid that she might lose her temper with somebody if she didn't step away from them all for a bit. It wasn't their fault, she was just frustrated.

Ainslie started to scream at the top of her lungs. Regan hurried back into the house. "Give it back!" the little girl was yelling. Josh had taken her stuffed bunny and was holding it above her head just out of reach. "Jump doggie," he was saying to the distraught child. Mark was nowhere to be seen, and Regan assumed that he was still sitting in the kitchen doing nothing. She didn't bother taking her boots off, just stomped across the dining room and snatched the bunny out of Josh's hands, "GO TO YOUR ROOM!" She roared at him. Then turning to Ainslie she handed her the bunny and said, "You too, go to your room." Ainslie started to protest but Regan put up her hand to stop her and said, "That was not a reason to scream," and pointed down the hall to the girl's bedroom. Ainslie threw her bunny to the ground and stalked off to her room.

"Where was Mark?" she wondered to herself. "Couldn't he have dealt with this little conflict?" The scene kept replaying in her mind and she couldn't help but feel bad for the way she handled it. There never seemed to be a right way when disciplining the children.

Regan felt drained and it took all of her energy to go back to the slider and sit in a dining room chair. She just slumped there with all of her outer wear still on, waiting for the water on the barbecue to boil. She had no intention of leaving the kids in their rooms; once breakfast was ready they would be released. She rubbed at her temples not because she had a headache, but because the action comforted her.

Mark came limping out of the kitchen and made his way over to Regan. Her head was hanging down and she was rubbing the sides of her head with her fingertips as she so often did when stressed. He put a comforting hand on her shoulder. When she looked up he could see the glossy look in her eyes, all wet and clearly on the brink of tears. The situation was weighing much too heavily on her. He wanted to tell her that it was okay, that everything was going to be alright. But the truth was he wasn't sure. If he had told her those things it would be a lie because he didn't believe them one hundred percent anymore so he didn't say anything. They stood like that for a little while, just looking at each other quietly.

The barbecue began to hiss, which meant the water was boiling, splashing liquid onto the heated cast iron surface. Regan once again hung her head and forced herself to stand up and deal with breakfast, leaving Mark standing alone in the dining room.

Funnily enough, his leg didn't hurt when he was standing on it. That could be because he balanced his weight on the opposite leg. It only seemed to really hurt when it was immobile, then he was forced to think about it, and when that happened, a burning sensation emanated from the wound. So he tried to stay active to avoid the horrible feeling.

Regan came through the slider with the boiling pot in her oven gloved hands and set it down on the dining room table. Mark had laid a folded up sheet out for her so that the pot wouldn't scorch the wood table top. She then quickly removed her boots and carried the pot off to the kitchen to make the oatmeal.

After a few minutes of mixing the oats into the water, she attained the correct consistency and called down the hall to her children, "guys you can come out for breakfast." Mark was hobbling over from the dining room and she just nodded to him to acknowledge him.

It was a very solemn breakfast. Nobody really said anything. Josh just poured a large amount of sugar into his bowl and Ainslie made a face at the sticky paste put in front of her. She dare not say she didn't like oatmeal as that would trigger more time alone in her room. She followed Josh's lead and added quite a bit of sugar to her meal.

Once finished, Josh asked, "Can I come out of my room now?" Sensing the opportunity Ainslie chimed in with a, "me too?" Regan nodded and said, "No more fighting." They both agreed and went out to the living room covering themselves with blankets. Regan hadn't thought about their rooms being cold and the fact that they had brought all of their bedding out to the living room. Instantly she felt bad for being thoughtless. A mother's guilt never ceases.

Mark gathered up some of the bowls, stopping in front of his wife to kiss her softly on the forehead. He put the bowls in the sink and headed back into the living room to join the children.

She stood in the empty kitchen alone weighing her options. Number one, get some water from the bathtub and clean the bowls. Number two, join the rest of her family in the living room for whatever activities they could come up with or number three, stay in the kitchen and have some alone time. She chose number three; sitting in the quiet kitchen she imagined a nice warm cup of tea in her hand. A newspaper would have been nice, but she could only find a leftover magazine in the bottom "junk drawer." Leafing through the magazine, she didn't read any of the articles, just looked at the different pictures of models or celebrities. They all seemed to be somewhere without snow. That was unimaginable to Regan right now. There was an ad for the Bahamas on one of the pages and Regan stared at it, slipping into a weird trance. She couldn't bring herself to turn the page. Her mind transported her to the white sandy beach she was looking at, closing her eyes she allowed the feeling to take her over.

Mark sat in the living room trying to occupy the kids. They didn't want to do anything, but they were restless. All the games were either dumb or lame and he was running out of patience with both of them until he had an idea. "Why don't you guys make a list of things you want to do when the snow melts?" Josh kind of shrugged, but Ainslie perked up, "can I draw what I want to do daddy?" she asked. "Of course," he replied. They gathered up some paper and pencil crayons and with their stretchy gloves still on their hands, set about their work. Mark thought about what he wanted to do once they were free. He came up with get out of the city for a week. Go somewhere and be pampered where you don't have to worry about making meals or entertaining children. The thought of going to a place that was hot seemed like an unreachable goal right now. What he would give just to feel the warm sun on his face, to swim with the kids and horse around in a pool. Drink weird tropical concoctions. Regan would be on board, he was sure of it.

"Look daddy," Ainslie was holding up her picture to show her dad what she had drawn so far. "It's you with Mickey Mouse ears on," she gave her dad a big toothy smile. He could see the space where her tooth used to be and smiled back at her, "that's very good honey."

Regan had snapped out of her little day dream and decided to clean up the kitchen. She couldn't really wash the dishes as to waste the water on anything other than drinking was crazy at this point. So she just gathered up any dishes that were lying around and stacked them neatly in the sink. There weren't that many as they had been using mostly paper plates to eat off of.

Then she used some paper towel to wipe off the counters, again she didn't allow herself to use any water so instead squirted some hand sanitizer onto the paper towel sheet and rubbed it across the counters. That would at least cut down on any germs or bacteria inhabiting the counter she hoped. The last thing they needed right now was for any of them to come down with a case of food poisoning or the flu. Their immune systems might be able to handle it, but having to warm the stones and make meals while under the weather would be a real chore. And she knew from past experience if one of them got sick, they inevitably all would have a turn.

Although there were dishes piled up in the sink, it made Regan feel a little better to have the kitchen tidied up. There were only so many things that she could control in her life right now. There was no reason for them to live like animals.

Mark could hear Regan moving around in the kitchen and the occasional clang of dishes hitting each other. It wasn't like an angry clean up sound, more of an, 'I'm on a roll' clean up sound. He was hoping that meant she was feeling a little better. The kids were busy working on their lists and Mark was feeling okay as well. His leg was propped up on the couch. Ainslie had insisted on a pillow under it, and it was a little uncomfortable at times, but he was able to ignore it for the most part. Mark was taking comfort in assuming the pain he was feeling was just a part of the healing process. The skin was busy repairing itself or something, but what did he know about medicine? He had changed the bandage this morning trying to be less of a burden to Regan. There was some pus and blood on the bandage, but he thought it looked like less than the day before. She had enough to deal with and he didn't want to add to it. He knew he would be fine; it would just take some time to heal.

Regan finished off the kitchen and headed out to the living room to see what everybody was up to. She was greeted by Ainslie's picture that the little girl displayed proudly for her. "This is you and this is daddy and we are at Disney World," she explained to her mother. "Oh, wow," Regan responded looking a little confused at her husband. "I asked them to think about what would be fun to do after the snow melts." Her husband explained Regan nodded in agreement of the little girl's idea. "That is a great idea," she replied, thinking of her earlier mental escape.

# 13 DAY SIX - AFTERNOON

*Just like a fire drill you and your family should put these ideas into practice. Every year there is an Earth hour, usually during the month of March, if you have not heard of this event shame on you, go and look it up online. It is an hour where everybody on the planet is encouraged to turn off every device that requires electricity to function. It doesn't sound like a big deal but I am ashamed to admit that it is not that easy. I suggest each year you use Earth hour as your trial run. This would be a good time to check those batteries in your radio. Just shut everything off, light some candles and talk to your family or your animals, whatever you have. You may be surprised what you learn about yourself, the people closest to you and Fluffy. – Survival Tips for the Urban Idiot*

No amount of practice could have prepared the Davis family for what they were currently enduring. The morning had marched by uneventfully. It was as though Mark and Regan were just waiting for the time to go by and at some point the power would come back on, or so they hoped. The only problem was, there were no guarantees that it would.

Regan was trying to motivate herself to start lunch. The usual issues plagued her; what would they eat? She didn't want to bundle up because her body ached, and she was cold and had been for days. On and on it went.

Ainslie had drawn three pictures. One was of the four of them at Disney World, another was the four of them on a beach, and the last was all of them walking on the surface of the sun. Maybe the cold was getting to her? Meanwhile, Josh had made a list that started out naming things like going to the zoo or the amusement park and morphed partway through into more of a Christmas list. He remembered his bike was too small for him and he would need a new one this year so he put that on. The thought of roller blading had appealed to him, so a new pair of skates went on the list. Even a trampoline and swimming pool showed up on his paper.

A dark cloud hung over the family for the majority of the afternoon. They all felt lazy and didn't want to do anything but lie around. A depression was affecting all of them. Gone were the desire to be entertained and the energy to try and make things a little more comfortable. They were replaced by an overwhelming bought of 'what's the point?'

For the first time since this had all began, nobody wanted to read. This brought a screeching halt to their night time ritual they had established over the past six nights. They all just got ready for bed and lay silently in the dark. Ainslie started to whimper so Regan put a comforting arm around her daughter. "It's okay, baby," she murmured to her youngest child. Josh had cuddled into her other side and her free arm pulled him closer to her. Mark was too far away to join them in the embrace and that brought tears to Regan's eyes. She just wanted her family close to her right now.

The candle she had lit burned dimly on the little stool above her head just as it had every night before. Regan stared up at the ceiling, watching the light from the candle flicker, casting strange shapes across the ceiling. In the dark, it was a scary display of distorted shadows and Regan was having difficulty figuring out where they were coming from. This left her feeling vulnerable. She tightened her grip on the children.

A short while later, both children had fallen asleep. She could feel the rhythm of their breath as they slept, but Mark was restless on the couch. He was moving around and sighing so she knew he was still up. Had he taken a Tylenol before he went to bed? She had no idea. He had started rejecting any help she offered when it came to his leg, insisting that it was fine. "Maybe he was just getting better," she thought. That made her wonder if he was okay, but she didn't want to risk waking the kids by asking him, so she continued to stare at the macabre scene unfolding on the ceiling.

Mark couldn't get comfortable. He tossed and turned on the couch and even though he was trying to stay quiet so as not to disturb his family asleep on the floor, he seemed unable to be silent in his restless state. His leg felt like it was on fire, and a deep throbbing had started earlier that afternoon inside the wound. He had considered on more than one occasion asking Regan to have a look at it, but the thought of worrying her, or it being beyond her limited medical knowledge was too scary for him. So instead, he endured.

The little tea candle that Regan had lit slowly sputtered out, extinguishing the only light available to him in the room. It didn't seem that dark with all of the blinds at the front window open though because the snow lightened the darkness of the night. He could make out large objects, but not the smaller details of the room.

Outside, the night was calm for the first time since the storm had begun. It was nice to not hear the wind howling for once, as it could sometimes be unnerving to listen to late at night. He didn't hear anything tonight.

Propping up his pillows elevated his head, giving him a good view of the street below. The windows were not iced over, which was a good sign. Maybe the temperature was finally starting to rise. All of the houses up and down the street were dark. It was peaceful outside. The snow had started to fall again, but they were slow, soft, large blobs as opposed to determined, sharp, little flakes. From experience he knew that this kind of precipitation could not go on for long.

He tried to close his eyes and sleep, but sleep wouldn't come. He looked over at Regan lying on the floor and thought that she had her eyes open, but it was impossible to tell for sure. Even if she was awake, he wasn't about to start up a conversation with her. The kids were flanking her on either side and any talking would definitely disrupt them.

If only he could flip over onto his stomach he thought, maybe that would do the trick and he would be able to get at least a little more comfortable. However, he couldn't do this as it would require him to pull his leg down from its propped up position. The pain he would endure shifting into a different position wouldn't be worth the reward of maybe being slightly more comfortable.

His frustration was reaching its peak and the need to punch something was overwhelming. He put a pillow over his face and grunted in annoyance into it. Sleep felt as though it would never come for him, and the more he thought about it, the further he got from it.

Putting the pillow back behind his head he burrowed into it when something caught his eye. He looked toward Mr. Fulton's house and saw a glow coming from the front window, what would have been the living room. Mark blinked his eyes as if to clear them and then rubbed them with the heels of his hands to be sure. The glow was still there and getting brighter. Mark lay very still as if whoever held that light would see him if he made any movement. The light shone brightest in the Fulton's living room, then moved to the left of the house, disappearing for a moment as it crossed the hall, blocked momentarily by the solid front door, then ending up in the kitchen. Mark just watched as the light moved around the house. He couldn't make out who it was inside for the darkness. The drapes were pulled, but they were made of a porous fabric that allowed outsiders to see in, probably left over from when Mrs. Fulton was alive. The light was in the kitchen for about ten seconds before it illuminated a figure. The height and stoop to the shoulders made it look like Mr. Fulton, but the figure clearly had two arms. Mark was confused and his arms were covered in goosebumps. He was positive that the man he was watching was not Mr. Fulton, but at the same time, it had to be. The way this person walked mimicked the old man's gait fairly closely, but there was something different about it, Mark couldn't quite put his finger on it, but the doubt was there.

And just like that, the figure and the light were gone and Mark was left to sit alone in the dark with his confusion. He shivered at the uneasiness that he felt. "Who was in the man's house if not Arthur?" he wondered. His mind was running wild, envisioning bandits in black ski masks ransacking the little house, knowing that nobody, not even a criminal would brave this weather for some worthless junk to be sold at a pawn shop later. Rational thoughts were not easily accessible at this time of the night.

Mark knew he was being silly and that he needed to get to sleep. After all, part of the healing process was rest, he remembered from grade nine health class. It was too late though; his mind was racing and overflowing with all kinds of different explanations for the light in the Fulton house. That was zombie Fulton who had managed to sew his arm back on, or a homeless person squatting in the impersonating the old man's home to wait out the storm. His favorite thought seemed to be the robbers as he kept coming back to that scenario. Sometimes there was a group, and others it was a lone gunman. In one case, he imagined a faceless man who broke into the house across the street. When he lifted his ski mask to reveal his identity, there was no nose or mouth, just skin and crazy, wild eyes. The thought never entered his mind that he had imagined the light and the figure, it was just too vivid.

Mark looked over at his family lying on the floor. He was pretty sure that Regan was asleep now. Her head listed to the left side and her arms gone limp around the children. Every once in a while she made a soft noise, not exactly talking, but more of a murmuring. Although he couldn't see her, he knew she looked beautiful. He would occasionally watch her sleep when he woke in the middle of the night. She looked so at peace, all of the tension in her shoulders and face gone. He wished she could always look that way, but the stresses of daily life had prevented that from happening.

Mark tried to remember what he would do at a time like this before the power had gone out. Usually he would be occupied by his phone. He would check his email, make notes of issues that were keeping him awake, or just play some mindless game to help tire himself out. He thought of his lifeless phone sitting in the kitchen drawer, now just an expensive paper weight. How quickly behavior can change when it has to.

The phone no longer mattered, watching the latest hot show no longer mattered. What did matter was surviving. It was ludicrous to think about the value shift that had taken place in their lives over the last five years. Technology had truly taken over, not as much as some other peoples' lives. Regan's sister for example had bought every gadget for her kids, occupying them so they would leave her alone in her hectic life. Her kids were no more than an accessory to her. And when they had enough, they would walk around saying the same thing, "I'm bored."

It made Mark feel a little sick to think of the future his children would have to be a part of. He had spoken to Regan quite a few times about escaping suburbia to go and live a real life where the kids could play outside and fish at a creek learning actual skills as opposed to being susceptible to carpal tunnel syndrome.

Regan had seemed receptive, having always been an animal lover; he had enticed her with thoughts of opening a kennel or boarding thoroughbreds. Although she didn't know the first thing about horses, the thought had intrigued her. But they had stayed. With each passing year it seemed less and less likely that they would do it. The kids were putting down roots and the longer they waited, the more difficult it would be to move them away from their friends. At least they got to have a little taste of the country when they went to Regan's folks place. Whenever they arrived at the house, the kids went outside and they didn't come back in until it was time to eat, leave, or escape unfavorable weather.

Mark smiled in the dark when he thought of last spring at the little house in the country. Ainslie, who was terrified of any kind of creepy crawly thing, was out in the mud catching frogs with Josh and Tyler, the boy who lived down the street from Regan's folks. The kids were filthy by the time they came in for something to eat.

Mark thought of his own childhood. He had lived in the suburbs too, but there were gravel pits and forests around them. On the weekend he would go with his older brother to the gravel pits and they would fish in the water, using corn as bait. He walked to school through the forest, collecting leaves along the way. This was how he first learned what poison ivy was. His brother had dared him to touch the plant, and Mark, not believing him, stupidly touched it and spent the next week with his arm covered in a very uncomfortable rash. He looked down at his right arm remembering the feeling; the arm gave no sign of ever having been damaged by the incident.

Turning on to his left side, Mark managed to relieve the numbness he was now feeling in his lower back. The couch was awful to lie on, and try as he might, it never fit right with the curve of his body. He looked towards the back window and saw a pair of green eyes looking back at him. He gasped and squinted into the dark, realizing that he was looking at a cat sitting under the barbeque. He felt bad for the little creature and tried to decide whether to let the little fur-ball into the house, but when he looked again, it was gone.

He used his good leg to kick off the blankets that were covering him. It felt as if they were made of lead and he could barely move. Despite the fact that the house was at a subzero temperature, he was warm and he wanted something to drink. He swung himself up to a sitting position and pulled his sweater over his head, then tossed it onto the arm of the couch. The t-shirt underneath was soaked through. Mark cursed Regan for forcing him to wear so many clothes. "The temperature must be rising." He thought to himself and felt Ainslie's neck to see if she was overheating too. She felt fine, not too cold and not too hot.

Mark got himself to his feet and had to stop a minute to gain his balance, putting most of his weight on the left leg. Once steady, he was able to navigate around the sleeping girl at his feet. He grabbed the flashlight that was lying on the floor next to the slippers and made his way to the kitchen.

He was thirsty and needed some water. His mouth was dry and his tongue felt as if there were a paste over it. He grabbed one of the bottles that Regan had refilled from the counter and drank half of the liquid before stopping to take a breath. It was room temperature, but he was starting to get used to drinking water that way. Regan had told him on more than one occasion that drinking ice cold water was not good for you. These days, it didn't seem like anything was good for you. He finished the rest of the bottle and put the empty container back on the counter next to the others.

With his hands on the counter to steady him, he closed his eyes and let his head fall back. His eyes burned and he knew that he needed to sleep. If only he could turn off his mind. He tried working out the kinks in his neck by rolling it from side to side, as if in some way that would relax him and help send him off to dreamland. His left eyebrow started to twitch and he brought his hand up to physically stop it.

He opened his eyes and looked around at the dark kitchen as if expecting to be transported somewhere else. Everything was the same. He rubbed at the eyebrow that had just been twitching to work out any weird tightened muscles that were there and put his hand on his wounded leg. His pants were damp from sweat as well. The thought of the temperature increasing was an exciting prospect and he looked forward to the sun being up. It wouldn't be long now; he guessed that it was about three in the morning. "Gotta get some sleep," he thought to himself and headed back to the living room to try again.

Retracing his steps, Mark tried to organize the sheet that covered the couch before lying down on it. Maybe that held the answer to his problem. All this time he just had to straighten the bedding he had been lying on. He knew that wasn't the case, but it wouldn't hurt to try and be as comfortable as possible.

Once satisfied with how his make-shift bed was made, he lay down on the couch. The sheets were cool and felt nice. He didn't bother to fix the blankets, leaving them slung over the top of the couch; he opted to cover himself with a cotton flat sheet instead.

Then he lay in the dark on his back again staring up at the ceiling, still wide awake. Maybe getting up wasn't such a good idea, but he had been so thirsty.

In the end, he picked up the novel they had been reading together and used the flashlight in an attempt to escape into the story. With any luck he would be asleep before he got a chapter in.

The book didn't work either. He read three chapters before giving up once again. The sky had started to lighten in the east and he knew that the morning would arrive shortly so he gave up. No use in trying anymore. Lying there, he waited for his family to wake up and the day to get underway.

# 14 DAY SEVEN - MORNING

*In today's modern world it is easy to forget how beautiful nature can be. Take advantage of this time by enjoying the silence, there will be no hum of electronics, whoosh of airplanes flying overhead or ringing of cell phones. Ahh, doesn't that sound nice? Sit in the backyard and see the truly greatest show on earth, the stars. Depending on the time of year and where you are you may even see a meteor shower or the Northern lights. Use this time to reconnect with your loved one's sharing stories of your family history. – Survival Tips for the Urban Idiot*

Regan opened her eyes and lay in the dark listening to her huddled family breathing almost in unison, as if they were one living organism. Her arms were still under the children and she could no longer feel her fingers. She flexed her hands forcing them into fists to get the blood flowing again. The sun would be up soon. She had gotten to know the lighting and the corresponding approximate times. She was not tired, but the thought of getting up was too much to bear; yesterday's overwhelming emotions had taken a toll. The cold would set in soon and they would need to warm the stones and come up with a plan for today.

She was sick of this. Sick of crappy instant meals, sick of the cold, sick of being cooped up. Maybe at some point throughout Mark's survivalist hobby she had thought it might be fun to have to actually survive. After having lived it, she would never fantasize about being one of the last people on earth again. As much as she hated living in the suburbs, feeling like you're the only one living in the suburbs was worse. It sucked; she just wanted a bath and a decent hot meal. Nothing canned or processed, just a chicken stir fry with lots of veggies and some brown rice would do the trick. Her mouth watered at the thought and her nose filled with the scent. She pulled up some memories of what cooking smelled like before all this, remembering the care that went into meals. She was sick of just choking something down for energy and trying to ignore the taste. If they made it through this, they were going on a vacation, she and Mark had agreed yesterday.

That struck a chord, "if they made it through this." That was the first time she had considered not making it. Even with everything that had happened so far, there had never been any doubt in her mind that they would survive. It seemed silly now to think that the possibility never entered her thoughts, seeing as how they were pretty sure three people on their street had died already. And with each passing day, the urge to survive grew stronger, encouraging riskier behavior.

The urge to pee had surfaced as well and she tried to ignore it. Caesar, sensing her consciousness, tried to plop himself down by her side, but ended up lying mostly on top of her. She shoved him over and opened the blanket so that he could snuggle into her. He was warm under the short coat and it was nice to feel him beside her. She put an arm over him, hoping that he would stay for a little while.

Her toes were numb and everything hurt just as it had the day before, and the day before that. Tears sprang to her eyes and a feeling of despair engulfed her. She couldn't fight it anymore. Exhaustion, pain and fear all took over and she sobbed into her pillow, trying desperately not to wake anyone.

She heard a sudden whirring sound she thought must have been the wind, but it wasn't coming from the windows or doors. The sound was coming from inside the house. A kind of dread filled her. What would today have in store for them? Her imagination running wild with thoughts of another broken window or the barbeque running out of gas, maybe the tub would freeze and they would no longer have access to water. She made a mental note to fill up some more bottles just in case.

The windows were so frosted over that she couldn't see outside. Did she really want to? There wasn't anything out there for her, just death, snow and ice.

There was a whoosh of air coming from somewhere and it dawned on her what the whirring noise was. "The furnace," she whispered to the darkness. Could it be? She threw the blankets off, frantically trying to escape, a renewed hope blooming in her, lighting her up with energy. She tumbled and fell over her own feet and Caesar, who was still caught in the layers of bedding she had been desperate to escape. Once she was free, she sprinted for the light switch, knocking aside the line of slippers that lay in a row on the floor. She flicked the little toggle up. The overhead light blazed to life, filling the room with an electric glow she had thought they would never see again. Her little family had stirred at the noise and were now staring up at her in disbelief; they had instantly woken up when the light came on. Their nightmare was over. They were going to be okay after all. Regan fell to her knees and came undone. Her brave face gone she cried hysterically into her hands, covering her face.

Outside, the street lights were blinking on, the sensors buried beneath the snow somewhere. The worst was over. All along the cul de sac houses lit up. They could see Mr. Fulton's house. It looked as though every light in the house was on. "Creepy," Regan thought to herself.

Regan had to adjust to the bright living room that surrounded her. Gathering herself up, she went into the kitchen and was greeted by the stove clock blinking twelve o'clock at her. She couldn't remember a time that she was so excited and deliriously happy. Her cell phone charger was in her room and she went to get it, almost running down the hall at the thought of talking to someone outside of these four walls.

Mark had heard Regan getting up; he had been awake all night and hadn't noticed the familiar sounds that were now buzzing around him. "We can finally go outside and start clearing the snow," he thought to himself. "We are finally free!" He thought of throwing wet clothes in the dryer, once they had cleared the driveway and the house becoming a warm vessel again. He felt the sting of tears threaten, but willed them away. This had definitely put their family's strength to the test, and he was glad that it was over now. Relief flooded through him. He hadn't wanted to worry Regan, but his leg was hurting now more than it had before and there seemed to be a horrible smell coming from the wound whenever he took off the bandage. He didn't want her to sew him up though, so he had kept quiet. He suspected she couldn't detect the scent because she had been sniffling for the past couple of days and her congestion was probably inhibiting her ability to smell.

Ainslie seemed a little confused by the commotion and sat looking at her dad. "What's the matter Ains?" he asked her. She shrugged her shoulders and said, "what do I do now?" He smiled and pointing at the TV said, "why don't you turn that thing on?" She looked behind her to where the TV was sitting over in the corner, looking at it as if she had forgotten all about it. Mark smiled, "wow, things have changed a lot in just six days," he thought to himself. Ainslie brought him the remote and wandered out of the room, he presumed to look for her mother. Mark lowered the volume so as not to assault their senses. He looked over at Josh who was still lying on the floor trying to wake up. Mark clicked over to the news.

Regan could hear the TV as she returned from her room, charger in hand. The thought of how quiet the house had been came back to her. Even with the kids playing, the absence of the TV droning on in the background had become a welcome change.

As she entered the living room, she saw the scene on the TV. Piles of snow everywhere, cars in ditches, people being rescued from buildings, cars, elevators, even planes, the last picture they showed was a line of three snow plows clearing the way. Regan looked out the front window. Some of her neighbors had already descended on their driveways, desperately digging them out, most of them probably in need of some supplies. She thought of her own cupboards, they probably could have gone a few more days, but they were scraping the bottom of the barrel at this point. The thought of their food supply reminded her that she had stumbled across some frozen waffles yesterday. She marveled at how easy it would be to pop them in the toaster. She left her husband watching the news and went to make a nice warm breakfast without having to dawn her outdoor gear.

Ainslie came back to the living room with her snow pants on. "Can we play in the snow now daddy?" she asked. "Yes honey, we can play in the snow." Ainslie did a little jump for joy and that was all Josh needed to hear, as he was now sitting up and blinking his eyes. "But first..." Mark said. Ainslie slumped her shoulders and leaned forward. "You need to eat breakfast," Mark finished. Ainslie straightened up and smiled at her dad, running over and throwing her arms around him. Josh tossed the covers off and bolted for the kitchen, followed closely by his sister. Mark could hear the familiar popping sound of the toaster as the waffles jumped away from the hot metal. There was also a bit of a commotion as the kids jockeyed for position. He turned off the TV and listened to the sounds of the house.

Regan put a waffle on a plate for each child and made them sit down. They were all hyped up about going out to play in the snow and quickly scarfed down their crunchy, toasted breakfast. Regan brought Mark a waffle and asked if he was okay to go outside. "I think I overdid it the last time," he said shaking his head by way of an explanation. She nodded in response and headed to the front door to get suited up.

Before putting her boots on, Regan returned to the living room and asked Mark, "do you need anything before we head out?" He shook his head, but said to her, "I think you should go out first and clear a path for the kids. Know what I mean?" She looked at him for a minute, and his eyebrows rose at her as if trying to will her to remember something. Then it clicked, she remembered the arm by the garage. "Oh yeah, I will." She turned to the kids who had all of their outdoor gear spread out over the floor. "Guys, I'm going to go out first and make a path for you." They both made an awwww, noise. "I'll be as quick as I can," she assured them. And with that, she put her boots on and wrestled her way through the front door.

She stepped outside into thigh-high drifts. The front path was covered and it was hard to decipher where it ended and the front lawn began. She would have to dig until the grass appeared, but first she needed to get to the garage and retrieve the snow shovels.

She tried to lift her legs out of the snow, but she was too short to clear it and she ended up falling face first into a pile that had a thin layer of ice hidden beneath the soft powdery surface. She smacked her cheek hard enough that she could tell instantly there was going to be a mark.

Once upright again, she forced herself through the drifts, using her gloved hands to push aside the icy layer as a swimmer would water. It wasn't easy, but she was able to make it to the garage. The sun was shining and that seemed to be melting the ice a little bit.

Standing at the garage door, she looked around for the arm. There was no trace of it, or even signs of where Mark had disturbed the snow. It would be buried down there somewhere, but she would need a shovel to find it.

She entered the code into the keypad for the garage door opener and heard the motor behind the large door start and strain, pausing for a minute. She gave it a kick and the door gave a mighty crack causing it to wobble and shake, then it rolled up out of her way. She had been afraid that it wouldn't open. She ducked under the slow-moving door as soon as the way was clear and found the adult snow shovel right inside the door for easy winter access. Turning back to the snow she had just walked through, the enormity of the situation hit her. The garage was half buried and would need to be dug out a layer at a time. The snow would be heavy and packed after so many days of freezing and thawing, it would not be an easy job. This was going to take a while.

Jabbing the shovel at the snow near the bottom of the pile, Regan hoped she would hit the arm. In all honesty, she had no idea where to look. She ended up carving out a space where she would have left it if it were her who had found it, but no luck. She tried a little more to the left, there was nothing there. After about ten minutes, she was sweating and had cleared the whole section in front of the garage, it was all piling up as mountains on the lawn.

Regan stood staring at the empty space. She had dug right down to the asphalt driveway and not found the arm. "Maybe it had blown away," she rationalized, but she knew that was impossible. Shrugging her shoulders she set about clearing the path she had promised.

By the time she made it to the front step, her arms were screaming, her knit cap was soaked with sweat, and her back was starting to ache. The snow weighed a ton, but she had accomplished her task. Looking over her shoulder, she admired her work. There was a path cut into the snow, no larger than her shovel's width, but it would serve its purpose.

She headed inside, needing some water and a reprieve from the strenuous exercise she had just completed. The kids greeted her as soon as she walked through the door. "Can we go out now?" Josh asked. He already had all of his snow clothes on, including one of his winter boots on his foot, the other at the ready in his hand. Regan looked at him and begrudgingly said, "okay, but stay on the path and dig out from there." He nodded enthusiastically and disappeared outside. Ainslie was pulling on her wooly jester hat and said, "Bye!" as she ran past her mother.

Regan sat on the bottom step catching her breath then she pulled off her own boots and plodded up the stairs to re-hydrate.

The TV was on, so she stuck her head into the living room and asked Mark if he was okay. He nodded, but he was staring intently at the television. More coverage of the storm was being splashed in HD across the screen. He was mesmerized by it. No doubt he would give her a full account later.

Upon entering the kitchen, she turned to where the now empty case of water stood. Frozen for a moment, she realized that the water would be running and grabbed a glass out of the cupboard and headed for the sink.

After downing two full glasses of water, she headed back down the stairs and put her boots back on. The driveway wasn't going to clear itself. Caesar sat at the top of the stairs and gave a little whimper. She looked at the big dog and said, "In a little while bud, you can go out, but we need to make it safe first." As if the dog would understand. She turned away gave her head a shake and thought to herself, "I'm losing it."

The kids were struggling to climb over the sides of the path, but kept at it, tumbling and laughing in the snow. They were so happy just to be outside. Regan was too. Breathing in the cool air, feeling the cold on their cheeks, it was different than the chill in the house. Maybe the thought that they could escape the cold by going in the now warming house helped.

Regan set to work shoveling off the front step, and after a little while, Josh joined her. They were able to clear the ten foot path and front step in about half an hour. Ainslie was not really any help, she was just being silly and playing around, but Regan didn't mind.

Once the path was clear, they all needed a break. "Why don't we go in for a warm up?" She suggested, to which Ainslie groaned and Josh started to speak, but Regan held up her hand to stop him and said, "I'll make hot chocolate." That was all it took. Both kids bolted for the door and ran inside the house.

It took a while for them to remove the layers of clothing, but they were chattering away the whole time about how many marshmallows they wanted in the warm treat. Regan wasn't sure if they even had marshmallows, but she wasn't about to put a damper on their fun.

Finally free of their outdoor things, they went upstairs to share their adventures with their dad, who still had the TV on. He muted it as soon as they entered the room. Regan hung up the wet things that had fallen off of the hook in the kids haste to get upstairs. Then, she carefully hung her own stuff up to dry.

She ascended the stairs slowly, her legs shaking a bit from the exertion of shoveling. The thought of a nice, hot cup of something propelled her forward.

In the kitchen, she pulled out four mugs from the cupboard, filled the kettle from the tap, and then pushed the button to turn it on. While the water was warming up, she opened the cupboard for the canned goods and found the hot chocolate immediately. Getting a tablespoon from the cutlery drawer, she poured a heaping spoonful into each mug, then went looking for marshmallows. They were in the canned goods cupboard on the top shelf; she had to use a chair to retrieve them. They were the campfire style, not the mini ones, so she got out a knife and chopped them up. They were a little stale and stiff when she tried to cut them, but she managed all the same. They would never notice when they were melting in the hot chocolate.

Once the kettle was ready, she filled all of the mugs, stirring the contents of each until they were all filled with a creamy, delicious smelling treat. Then, placing all of the cups on a tray, she carried them into the living room to serve up to her family.

Mark turned the TV off as she entered the room and propped himself up into a sitting position. "Oh, hot chocolate," he said surprised. She noticed that he still seemed to be babying that leg and wondered if there was something that he wasn't telling her.

*In the event of a power outage no matter what the season the most important thing is to remain calm. Keep your loved ones close and encourage them to keep calm as well. In our modern age I think we tend to panic a little prematurely- Survival Tips for the Urban Idiot*

Regan took advantage of the time and threw all of their outdoor gear into the dryer so that they would be ready after lunch to go out and complete the job of shoveling the driveway.

By now, the whole street was out desperately trying to clear the snow. The sun had come out and was shining down on everyone. A few people had turned their faces into the rays, enjoying soaking up the much needed vitamin D.

Mark stood at the window looking at his neighbors outside. They all seemed to be out there except Mr. Fulton and the twins. He was staring at Mr. Fulton's house when he saw a light go off in what would be the kitchen. Mark had never been in the little house across the street, but he knew the layout of the bungalow. The front window on the left was the kitchen and the window on the right was the sitting room. He watched the house for a few minutes and resolved the outage to a bulb going out when the sitting room light went out. He stared intently at the house and thought he saw the shadow of a figure in the hallway, from as far away as he was it was hard to tell. He stayed put, waiting for something else to happen.

After about ten minutes, Regan appeared beside him and asked, "whatcha looking at?" Startled, he said, "I thought I saw someone in Fulton's house." He reported. She followed his stare and tried to see what he was looking at. With the reflective snow, it was hard to see anything and she had to look away after a little while because her eyes started stinging. "Do you think it's him?" she asked. He looked at her, realizing he had not even considered that possibility. "I don't know," he wondered leaning against the arm of the couch suddenly very tired.

"Well I am going to get lunch started, are you okay?" Mark had turned pale and looked weak; he nodded in response as if words were suddenly too much of an effort for him. She helped him get back to a comfortable position on the couch. He felt warm to the touch and Regan went to get him some Tylenol and lunch.

The kids were lying on the floor; they had taken over the TV and were watching some cartoon character get himself into a ridiculous situation that a normal person would be able to solve in about five minutes.

Regan busied herself making KD for lunch, there was no milk left so she just used the last of the butter which seemed to work. She knew that they would need to get to a grocery store by tomorrow if they wanted to return to a normal meal plan. In reality, clearing the driveway meant she could get real food, and that is exactly what she had in mind, even if it meant driving to the next county. From what the news was saying, the local stores were in a real mess; defrosted meat that had spoiled, shelves had been looted, some of them looked like they had been in a war zone so she might have to drive a little ways. It would be worth it though! The thought of a real meal almost seemed too good to be true.

Mark was lying on the couch when Regan brought the lunch in. She was starting to worry about him, he didn't look so good. She placed his bowl on the arm of the couch and went back to the kitchen for a glass of water and the Tylenol that she had forgotten. He was able to eat a little of the pasta, then he downed the Tylenol. She got him a blanket and covered him up hoping that after some sleep he would be feeling better.

Heading downstairs, she could hear the dryer thumping from all of the coats and hats in it and she smiled to herself at the fact they had the electricity back. "You really don't know what you have until it's gone." She thought to herself.

The kids came running when Regan called. They grabbed all of their items from the pile she had taken out of the dryer and left at the front door. The coats had still been a bit damp on the outside, but everything else was toasty and warm. They were ready in no time and headed out to play in the winter wonderland. Regan checked on Mark before going outside. He was asleep on the couch so she didn't disturb, him quietly closing the front door behind her.

Mark had fallen into a feverish, fitful sleep plagued with nightmares. He dreamt that someone had come in the back slider and crept up beside him, just staring down at him while he slept. When he woke up, Caesar was there panting over him, waiting expectantly for who knew what. "Go," he commanded the dog, and Caesar obliged. Mark was soaked in sweat and still felt exhausted so he lay in the quiet living room listening to the far off voices of his children playing in the snow drifting back to unconsciousness.

Josh was able to help Regan clear most of the driveway. She was only really worried about getting one car out so they opted for the side with the minivan that way if something happened and they needed to get somewhere they could all fit comfortably in it, dogs included. The other side could be finished tomorrow, the focus right then was freedom. Regan watched the front window periodically for a sign of her husband. She was starting to worry about him, was he hallucinating? She turned toward Mr. Fulton's house, which was dark now. "That's weird," she thought to herself. "When the power came on it looked like every light had been left on, now the house is dark." She watched the house for a minute as if she thought Mr. Fulton would come bursting out of the front door, but nothing happened. She shook her head. What was she doing? He wasn't in there, she needed to focus on the task at hand and get back to work, they weren't finished yet.

In his next dream, Mark had been impaled by the birch tree that had come through the master bedroom. He tried to get away, but the tree had come to life and whenever Mark tried to pull himself free, the tree would drive a long sharp branch into his leg. The pain felt real, and he cried out more than once. Somehow, he had gotten himself away from the tree only to wind up in a darkened ally with what he thought were dogs surrounding him. All he could see were the glow of their eyes and bared white teeth. When he turned to run, his legs were stuck to the spot and he could only move his upper body. He flailed uselessly and tried to claw at something to use as a lever. He knew they were going to attack, he could smell it in the air, but he couldn't get away. Fear rose in the back of his throat. The dogs were growling and descending on Mark. He held up his arms in front of his face to fend them off while he let out a scream. Once again, he woke in a cold sweat.

A rumbling noise came from the top of the street; everyone stopped what they were doing and turned towards the sound. A huge snow plow was forcing its way down the street. Of course, compared to the snow it didn't look that big, but you could tell it was one of the ones you would see clearing the highway. All of the neighbors dropped whatever was in their hands and started to cheer, clapping and whooping at the sign of the truck. They would finally be free, able to leave the prison of the street and start living again. The excitement was contagious and Regan turned toward her house in time to see Mark standing at the front window. He looked pretty disheveled. He was staring down at the house across the street. Regan followed his gaze over to see someone standing at the living room window, peeking through the blinds in Mr. Fulton's house. Maybe he was okay and the arm they found had belonged to someone else. That should set Mark's mind at ease.

Then the gravity of the situation hit her. The plow was going to push all of the snow that was covering the street back into the place that she had just spent the majority of the day clearing. "Oh shit," she thought to herself not sure if she had anything left to keep going. She could see people already jumping back away from the avalanche that was now encroaching on them. She turned to the kids and yelled to them to move back. They were almost at the foot of the driveway and didn't hear Regan so she marched up behind them and grabbed both of them by the back of their winter coats, pulling them to safety. They realized what she was trying to do and ran up the driveway out of the way just before a mountain of snow chased after them up the length of the driveway.

When Regan looked up again, Mark was gone. She immediately turned to Mr. Fulton's house. There was no sign of anyone looking through the window anymore. The street was now clear and she could reach the other side, but the snow was still too deep at the Fulton's as no one had shoveled his driveway. What did she think she would find at the house? "It's not my problem," she told herself and left her suspicions outside.

Josh and Regan made quick work of the snow plow residue as the truck had completed the hard part of breaking up the ice crust. Once they were finished, they headed back in the house. It took some convincing to get Ainslie to join them, but her cheeks were so pink Regan was starting to worry. The sun was going down and the temperature felt like it was dropping again, so Regan promised another mug of hot chocolate and some cartoons. Ainslie held out for a board game instead of cartoons. "Interesting…" her mother thought to herself.

In the house, they brushed the snow from their clothing and ensured everything was hung up to dry. Regan tiptoed through the wet carpet to the stairs and found a very sweaty and pale Mark lying on the couch, just staring off into space. She touched his forehead with the back of her hand and discovered he was burning up. She touched his arm, "Mark?" he didn't react to her voice. "Honey?" she tried again. He blinked his eyes and turned towards her voice, giving her a very weak smile. "I think we should get you to the hospital." She decided calling to Ainslie to fetch his coat and Josh to help her prop him up and get his boots on. He didn't resist, just let them do what they wanted to him.

Regan rushed out to start the van. She hoped there was enough gas to get them to the hospital. It was a good ten minutes away. She noted that there was a quarter tank left, and figured they would be fine. Heading back into the house, Josh was helping Mark down the stairs and Ainslie was holding his coat ready for him when he reached the door. They bundled him into the van and set off.

The streets were deserted, but clear, and Regan silently thanked god for that. Everything looked different to her. The same streets she drove down every day seemed somehow alien to her now. Maybe it was being off of them for a few days. It didn't really matter right now as she sped towards the hospital.

They made great time and unloaded Mark at the emergency room door, putting him in a wheelchair. Regan said to Josh, "take him inside where it's warm and stay with him. I'm just going to park the van."

She climbed the parking garage ramp and ended up having to park on the second level since the first level was reserved for employees. She quickly got Ainslie out of the van and practically dragged her to the stairs. Thinking better of it, she went to the elevator and hit the button, anxiously awaiting the car's arrival.

They were back at the emergency room door in no time, and wheeling Mark into the triage area. The hospital was deserted; Regan had never seen it like this. One nurse, where normally there would be three, was sitting at the front desk and she looked up when they came through the door. She waved them over, "hi folks, what's going on today?" she asked.

Regan pushed Mark forward and told the nurse what had happened. She took his blood pressure, temperature and listened to his heart. "Can I see the wound?" she asked. Mark needed help rolling up the leg of his pajamas but when he did the nurse removed the bandage and it was clear that he was in trouble. Green puss was oozing out of the half closed wound, the crazy glue had only bonded some of the skin and the flesh around it was red and puffy. "Oh god," Regan exclaimed.

The nurse quickly took his information and wheeled him off to the Rapid Assessment Zone. Regan tagged along with the kids and got them settled in the waiting area where the TV was on. The nurse there changed the channel for them and found some cartoons.

Mark was transferred to a gurney where he laid waiting for help. His eyes were looking around wildly; it was as if he didn't know where he was or what was going on. Regan held his hand to comfort him.

A nurse appeared and took his temperature, blood pressure, and checked his heartbeat again. When she was finished, she handed him a little cup with a Tylenol in it and went to get some water.

Mark held the little cup in his hand, but he looked so wobbly that Regan took it off of him for fear that he might drop the pill. The nurse returned with the water and adjusted the narrow bed so that he was sitting comfortably. He started to look better already. Maybe it was just the relief of knowing he was getting help that made him feel better.

Mark felt awful. Now he knew what his grandmother meant when she said that someone looked like death warmed over because that was how he felt. He laid on the gurney; his leg feeling like it was on fire. Once the doctor looked at him, he would be able to go home and curl up on the couch again. That was all he wanted to do, just go to sleep. He couldn't though because everyone kept bugging him. His eyes would close for a minute and Regan was poking him to take a pill then he would get to rest again and the nurse was sticking a thermometer under his tongue. He wanted to yell at them to leave him alone, but he didn't have the strength.

The doctor came in and had a look, mentioned something about a local and disappeared again. The nurse was talking to Regan and she looked worried, but Mark didn't care. The nurse gave him a shot right next to the wound and he gasped at the pain, but within a few minutes he felt nothing and was able to relax.

Regan watched as the nurse injected a local anesthetic into the wound, "it will take a few minutes to take effect, and then the doctor will come in and clean it out." She placed a reassuring hand on Regan's arm as she walked away.

The kids were within earshot and she just had to stick her head out of the curtain to see them. Josh had taken off his coat and piled his outer wear on the chair next to him. Ainslie was reading a book she had found amongst the magazines strewn across the make-shift coffee table.

The doctor returned and said, "do you want to step out? This might get nasty." She looked at her sleeping husband and shook her head. How could she leave him in such a vulnerable position? The doctor took out a scalpel and cut the skin that had held with the crazy glue. The wound opened up revealing dark red flesh underneath. The doctor squeezed a bottle of saline into the cut and some greenish brown fluid came out. He touched the flesh inside. "There is something in there." Regan managed to tear her gaze away from the grotesque scene to look at the doctor. "We are going to need to get him in for an X-Ray; I need to know what I'm dealing with," and he disappeared again.

Regan stood looking at her dozing husband. A few minutes later, he was being wheeled to his X-Ray. Regan went to tell Josh to watch Ainslie and that she would be right back, but was surprised to see an elderly woman perched in the chair next to Ainslie with her head bent down, hiding her face from Regan's view. With the sound of Regan's approaching footsteps, the woman turned. To Regan's amazement, she was looking into the face of Norma Reid, one of the twins from across the road. Her shock consumed her and Regan broke down in tears. Josh, seeing his mother upset, went to her asking, "mom are you okay?" This was a silly question as she was clearly not. Regan smiled through her tears and hugged Norma. "You're okay," she whispered in the woman's ear. Norma, shocked and a little embarrassed at Regan's greeting, pushed the distraught woman an arm's length away, and looking puzzled, said, "well of course I am, been at the damn hospital for six days because of Nina's hip."

The twins, Nina and Norma, it turned out had not died in the fire. They had gone to the hospital the night it all started as Nina was having problems with her hip, and had broken out in a fever. It had taken Norma nearly five hours to get her sister to the emergency room that night, but she made it. Slippery conditions and blinding whiteouts made for a long trek. What they didn't know was, in their haste to get to the hospital, they had left the barbeque on and unattended.

Regan felt horrible, but she had to let Norma know what had happened. "Oh Norma," by now her tears had dried. "There was a fire. Your house burned to the ground." Norma's face had been so confidant a few moments earlier now turned to a mask of despair. "Oh no," she gasped. She sat down hard in one of the hospital waiting area chairs stunned. " I have to go let Nina know." Scrambling to her feet, the elderly woman walked away down one of the brightly lit hospital hallways, disappearing around a corner as Regan watched her go.

When Mark came back from X-Ray, he wasn't looking much better. What they found in the leg was an inch long piece of glass embedded in the cut. They were able to remove it and the doctor told Regan that he was very lucky he missed the femoral artery by half an inch. She knew that if he had hit that, he would have died three days ago.

They had to stitch up his leg and give Mark a prescription for antibiotics, and then they were free to go. Regan was relieved, and the kids were quite happy to have a little adventure. They loaded Mark back into the van, putting him in the middle captain's chair, and made him as comfy as possible, and then Regan headed for a fully functioning grocery store. It was dinner time and they were all starving. On route, they passed an open McDonald's and ended up stopping to pick up dinner for the evening. Regan decided the groceries could wait until the next morning and went into the little convenience store next to the restaurant grabbing a few provisions.

They arrived home tired and hungry, so they ate their food quickly. Mark couldn't eat all of his, so Josh and Ainslie helped. Then they got their dad cozy on the couch, being extra careful when propping up his leg. The colour in his face had come back and he didn't seem as drowsy anymore.

After dinner, Regan took the dogs for a walk. They were so excited to be out in the snow; a few times Regan had to yank on the leashes to keep them on track. She only went up the street and back, it was starting to get cold again with the sun down. Each house she passed had lights on and that meant the occupants were safe and warm. She looked across the street and Mr. Fulton's front light was on again. She got goose bumps up her arms. Somebody was definitely in the house, but whom? It had to be Mr. Fulton, but then whose arm had they stumbled across, and where had it gone? The driveway of the house across the street was still inaccessible, otherwise Regan might have braved a knock on the front door. She knew they would eventually find out, but she was still creeped out, and part of her didn't want to know.

She went up her driveway and into the warm and cozy house. The kids had changed into their pajamas and were setup on the floor watching TV. "Can we sleep in here one more night?" Josh pleaded. How could she refuse?

Once everyone was ready, they turned off the TV and read from their book. That night, everyone slept soundly.

*Well, that is all I have. Remember, this information is a guideline not a guarantee. If you find yourself in one of these unfortunate incidences I hope the fact that you have read these little tidbits helps you navigate through it and the situation turns out to be nothing more than a minor inconvenience and a nice family memory because you were ready. —Survival Tips for the Urban Idiot*

The storm took its toll on the whole city. The hydro company was able to complete the repairs to the grid by the end of that week. Regan and Mark watched as the poles were erected one by one, two streets over from their back window. The family cheered as the last one was put in place. They had opted for cement poles this time as opposed to their wooden predecessors. Regan couldn't help but feel vulnerable, she was at the mercy of the weather and if it had decided to start snowing again they could possibly have ended up in the dark once more, delaying the workers from finishing the job.

Sunset Place had been one of the last streets to be brought on line. Regan and Mark figured it was because they didn't have any important figures living there and the street was a court, giving no access to any major roads, so it was not at the top of the essential road list.

Once the power was up and running and everything seemed to be back to normal, the stories began to surface around tragedies suffered during the storm. It was a relief to know that most people were safe and relatively unscathed from the event, but then there were the ones that weren't so lucky. Those were the stories that hit a little too close to home for Regan and Mark.

Regan's boss had ended up trapped in his car when he pulled off the snowy road with the intention of waiting out the blinding snow squall he had driven into. It had become impossible for him to see anything, and the police presumed he thought it would be safer to stay put for a little while as opposed to risking driving with no visibility. This was probably the worst thing he could have done, as a passing snowplow at work could have demolished his car as it sped past, not seeing the automobile as it was buried under the snow. Alas, this was not his fate.

After a few hours, the Honda Civic he was driving became very cold and he started the car for some heat. The falling snow and freezing rain had been thick and were falling fast, encasing the car in a make-shift sarcophagus that, in the end, caused the carbon monoxide expelling from the muffler to become entrapped in the small space the car was occupying. The snow was falling so fast that the car fumes and heat could not melt the frozen water quick enough, poisoning the air within the automobile. He went peacefully to sleep before the air killed the poor man in his car. Regan went to his memorial to pay her respects. This was where she learned the man only had one family member remaining, his sister. She was upset, but had her husband and three children for comfort. The children were distraught, but Regan couldn't tell if it was from being in a room with a dead body or if they had really cared for their uncle. She hoped it was the latter.

Disturbed by the fact that she had known so little about this man she had interacted with on a daily basis, Regan vowed to change her ways. Bob had shared little about himself, often just listening to his employees. As a result, she was a little disappointed that, of the ten people Bob had managed, only her and one other woman named Cheryl showed up to his memorial. He had always been good to Regan and showed great understanding when it came to her family. She was glad he hadn't suffered in the end.

Mr. Fulton was a whole other complicated tale. It turned out the shadows and figures that Regan and Mark had seen in Fulton's home were not the old man or his ghost after all. A week before the storm started, his son had returned to visit his father. Regan and Mark were both relieved to learn that they had not been hallucinating.

Fulton junior had become destitute and had nowhere else to go, so he reached out to his estranged father for help. The old man had let his son stay with him, maybe out of guilt or perhaps his own loneliness, no one really knew. He hadn't let anyone else know that the younger Fulton was staying with him. Although, who would he even share that information with? He was rarely seen on the street during the winter, and that was the only way he would socialize with anyone, just casual conversation on the street with neighbors.

The younger Fulton had become frustrated at the lack of preparation his father had taken when the power went out, and threatened the old man to get provisions or suffer physical abuse at his son's hand. He forced the old man out into the cold to get whatever items they were running short on, which turned out to be everything. That was why he had shown up at Regan and Mark's house trying to steal the water. Had he just been honest they would have helped him, but for some reason he didn't feel he could.

Knowing what Mr. Fulton had been dealing with did little to ease Regan and Mark's guilt at turning the old man away. How were they to know that he was in any danger? If he had just swallowed his pride he may still be alive.

The third day of the outage hungry and growing ever more frustrated the son pushed his father out of the sliding back door and locked it. The police deduced the elder Fulton had become disoriented in the back yard and lost his way in the blowing blizzard unable to push through the heavy drifting snow that at times would have been up to the old man's shoulders, succumbing to the elements. His son found him the next morning one hundred feet from the back door of his own house frozen to death.

Fulton's son didn't bother to check on his father and ensure that he was indeed dead; he just left his father's body out in the cold to be buried day after day under layer upon layer of fresh powder, with no remorse.

To add insult to injury once the son had run out of food he ventured out to the corpse and carved some meat off of his father surviving the remaining days by literally living off of his dad.

The police only became aware of the old man's demise when the neighbors that back onto Mr. Fulton's backyard saw the old man slouched over in the snow one sunny day two weeks after the power had been restored to the house.

The man was cold and unremorseful when confronted with the death of his father. He was taken into custody and charged with a number of crimes. It was all anybody on the street could talk about. As much as the street didn't care for Mr. Fulton, the fact that someone could treat another human being so terribly struck a chord and the neighbors banded together to give him a proper send off. Raising money for a beautiful wreath and almost everyone attended the service that was organized.

The disembodied arm resurfaced in a snow bank down the street when the thaw set in and it did turn out to in fact belong to Mr. Fulton. During the storm a dog from two streets over had been able to escape his yard after being left in the cold while his owners went out the night the whole fiasco started. The owners were unable to return home and care for the animal, leaving the canine to his own devices. He happened upon Mr. Fulton's corpse and made a meal of him, returning a few times to take bites out of him, and then severing the arm, carrying it off, and burying it in the snow for later. Animal control had rounded up the dog and returned it to its rightful owner. A few days went by and the people brought the dog to the city shelter as he had become unruly now able to escape his yard the poor dog was becoming a danger to the community and he would no longer listen to the owners. The shelter workers had experienced the same issues having the dog snap at employees as well as families that were potential adoptees for the dog who were visiting the facility. Ultimately, after attempts at rehabilitation failed the decision was made to put the animal down.

The twins were devastated at losing everything, but at the same time, they were relieved that they hadn't been in the home at the time of the fire. The basement had been relatively untouched by the blaze, but having no house to protect the area left it open to damage from the elements of the storm. All of their photos and items their mother had left them were destroyed. The ladies were staying at the Holiday Inn while the insurance sorted out their claim. It was bound to take a long time.

Regan's parents had suffered a little more than was initially thought. The wood they had prepared the summer before had gotten wet, and when her father used it to warm the house in the wood stove, it smoked up the little house, forcing her parents to open the windows. Her father had indeed dropped a wooden log on his foot; however, it was not a clean break as her sister had claimed. The bone had shattered, and it would take three surgeries to repair. Even after all that, the doctor said he would never get full mobility back. He had to deal with the pain for two days during the storm while her mother focused on trying to keep them warm and fed as well as manage his pain with Tylenol and some codeine she had left over from a root canal. It was a good thing they were only out for a few days as there was no way they would have made it the whole seven that Regan and Mark had. Since then, Mark has built a little wood shed for them to keep the fuel dry, in the event this happens again.

Samantha was finally able to come home from sunny Florida. In her absence, a pipe had burst in her basement that filled the space with a foot of water, which then froze. This damaged her pool table, carpet, and the furniture down there. Her insurance company refused to pay for the damages stating that it was an act of god that caused the storm and ultimately the damage so they didn't cover those types of incidences. She had started the process of suing them and in the meantime had to have the water pumped out of her home and the furniture scrapped.

The birch tree was removed from Regan and Mark's bedroom window, and the glass and frame were replaced. It took a little while, but the house had been put back together and the family had returned to their usual routine, but with one exception. A for sale sign now stood on the lawn. Friday nights had also change a little; the family would now huddle together in the living room with their sleeping bags and have a 'camp out.' This was something that they came up with to stay close to each other. Regan had not been able to sleep normally since the whole ordeal and seemed to be suffering from some post-traumatic stress, frequently waking up in a cold sweat, and she had gotten it in her head that the only way to feel better would be a fresh start in a new home that was equipped to handle any future events of this nature.

She had also developed a strong affliction to being a part from her family. She ended up impulsively quitting her job to be a stay at home mom, not telling Mark of her plan until afterwards. Contradicting what she had originally thought at her boss's memorial of getting to know the people around her better, she was instead becoming withdrawn. The house they purchased would have to be cheaper than the current dwelling they were living in as without Regan's income, they would have to downsize.

Mark had suffered his own setbacks from the experience. His leg had healed fairly nicely given the circumstances, but the muscle damage caused by the infection had affected the way he walked. He would spend the rest of his life with an obvious limp. Athletics were restricted as well. He could no longer run, but skating seemed unaffected, so he played hockey when he could.

Regan had become distant and suffered overwhelming

depression. Mark tried to be there for her, but he was starting to worry that she needed professional help and possibly medication. She disregarded this fear when he shared it with her, insisting that she was fine and what they were experiencing was normal. "I just need a little time, and then I'll be good," she would tell him. It had only been a few months, maybe she was right. All he could think though, was that something had to give. It was becoming unbearable to be around her. Her misery sucked any joy out of the room she was in.

Ainslie and Josh seemed to recover fully from the incident. Going back to school and returning to normal had helped, although Ainslie's teacher had reported seeing the girl with her thumb stuck in her mouth on a few occasions causing the other kids in her class to taunt her and call her names.

Josh, unbeknownst to anyone, had started to sleep with Caesar in his room and a large kitchen knife under his bed. Although his parents had tried to shield the kids from what happened, he had heard stories at school of murders and break-ins on other streets as well as the local stores that had been looted. It was all over the news anytime the TV was on. He didn't want to take any chances.

Generators, wood stoves and alternative energy should have become hot commodities in the town, but as is the case with people, they slipped right back into their old, ignorant ways, as if the same disaster couldn't occur twice in their life time. Everybody seemed to be on the same page when it came to the next time this happens. Regan paid attention to the fact that they had become more dependent on technology and this was the first time it had happened since the town had been established one hundred years earlier.

The mayor declared February 10th, as "storm day" and dubbed it an unofficial holiday. Businesses were allowed to close their doors or alter their hours if they wished and the following year there would be a memorial service downtown for those lost during the blizzard.

All in all, 500 people ended up dying as a result of the storm. Well, it was actually 486 and most of them were elderly and they just weren't prepared to go seven days without electricity. The majority had succumbed to the elements or starvation. One woman, believed to suffer from Alzheimer's, had wandered out into the snow in a cotton, short-sleeve dress and flip flops. They found her in a snow bank at the foot of her daughter's driveway; she had walked from her apartment two streets over and almost made it to her destination. What a sad thought it was to die within sight of your target. A good deal of the stories were like hers. There was one about a man who had passed away as a result of not having someone to share body heat with. He had bundled up in all of his clothes and with all the threadbare blankets he could find, but it wasn't enough. An investigating journalist had asked a doctor how the man could have survived and the doctor suggested if he had someone to share heat with he probably would have made it.

"I survived the GREAT blizzard," shirts started to pop up just a few weeks after the storm with the proceeds going toward a statue the community was lobbying to have erected in Gage park in the downtown core. The statue would be of a snow plow next to a snow bank. What would that look like? Regan couldn't imagine. It seemed that most of the population wanted to commemorate the storm.

The more the city seemed to band together, the more

left out Regan felt. "Why couldn't everybody just get on with their lives?" She thought. Ainslie and Josh weren't allowed to partake in any events related to the storm. Regan thought everyone was taking advantage of a bad situation and exploiting the people who had lost something or someone.

Life went on in the little city and once the spring came, all was forgotten. It seemed as though everyone had finally moved on, but there was an underlying ugliness. As if they all shared a dirty little secret. Years from now, the storm would be nothing but a memory for most of the inhabitants. After all, terrible tragedies were taking place all over the world every day. Why would a winter storm in a small city be a historic event to the rest of the nation? The town had a record number of people move out that year. The population dropping by one hundred, could it have been the storm? Nobody really knew.

When the time came to build the statue, city hall had conducted a town meeting to agree on the design. The proposed design upset the town's folk and they were outspoken about it. The artist having been offended by their reaction walked away from the project, and in the end, the memorial was never built. The following year, no one recognized February 10th.

The                                                                     End

Nicole Paton Schofield is an award winning amateur photographer, busy mom of two, and a marketing associate at a large public company. She is currently enrolled in the University of Toronto's writer's craft course and is a graduate of the world-renowned Sheridan College. She resides in the city of Mississauga just outside of Toronto, Ontario Canada with her two teenage children, her husband of almost twenty years, their two dogs, Sam and Buddy, along with their grey tabby cat Cocoa.